DELMAR

ARCHER'S DYNASTY BOOK 1

KATHI S. BARTON

World Castle Publishing, LLC
Pensacola, Florida
Copyright © Kathi S. Barton 2021
Paperback ISBN: 9781955086288
eBook ISBN: 9781955086295
First Edition World Castle Publishing, LLC, May 24, 2021
http://www.worldcastlepublishing.com

Chapter 1

"Del, I'm not sure what you think is going to happen with you just staring at your computer, but you're supposed to be working." He grinned at his boss and friend, David Soldier. "You're not nearly as charming as you might think. In fact, I've never told you this before, but I think you're downright ugly."

"Have you once looked in the mirror? I'm sure people would tell you it's a face that only a mother could love, but you did find a woman to marry you. I can only hope that Apple never has her eyes checked, or you're going to be in deep trouble when she gets a good look at you." He turned his screen off when he realized it was getting later than he'd thought. "I got the specs done on the equipment we talked about and made copies of it all for tomorrow. There are any number of plants around that could do it, but as we talked about before this project, we have to go local."

"We're doing well, and it would be good to help out someone that is just starting out as we were doing a few years back." He agreed, and tomorrow he was going to visit three of the local places to see if they could come up with the design that would be used in hospitals across the world. "You think any of them will be large enough to handle the kind of needs we'll have with this?"

"I haven't any idea. But what I do know is that we won't know for sure until we ask them. Also, you're taking Judy with you. She's been wanting to branch out in what she does, and she'd rather go with you than me." He asked him why. "I don't know. I thought it was because she didn't like me, but she assured me that she thought I was a great boss. But she'd rather be around you."

Going home wasn't nearly like it used to be. He'd been living with his mom for the last few years until a few months ago. Now she was out on a cruise and wouldn't be returning for a few days. She'd taken a job on a cruise line and was working as a cook. Getting to enjoy the cruise life seemed to suit her a great deal. Using his key, he made his way to his room to switch into something much more comfortable than a suit and then pulled out his menus.

With his mom gone, he hadn't had a good homecooked meal in ages — at least it seemed like it to him. Ordering a dinner to be delivered was how he'd been doing it for the last few weeks. Usually, he would order double so that he'd have enough for his dinner the next night and his lunch tomorrow. Tonight he ordered himself a sub and a bag of chips.

As usual, there was nothing on television, and he ended up getting on his computer and working more on the plans. It was nearly three in the morning when he finally made his way to his room, so exhausted that he didn't know if he was going to make it to his bed. Living at home at his age wasn't something he'd planned, but it had worked out for his mom and him.

The pounding at his door startled him. Falling out of his bed, the pounding never stopped. At least until whoever it was found the doorbell, and then it was just one continuous chime as he stomped his way to the door. Jerking it open, he grabbed the hand that was still pressing on it and pushed it away.

"What the fuck do you want?" His mind registered two things at once. This was a woman, and he was naked. "It's — I have no idea what time it is, but since it's dark, I can only assume that — "

"Can you get some clothes on? Christ, you're

naked as a jaybird." She looked at his face when he crossed his arms over his chest and stared at her. "Seriously? You're going to be all macho on me?"

"You woke me up from a dead sleep. You take what you get. What do you want?" She told him the time. "What do you want at five-thirty in the morning?"

"You didn't make an appointment with my firm." He didn't even bother asking her what the hell she was talking about but turned his back on her to go back to bed. "Do you have any coffee? I missed my breakfast too."

"Like I give a shit." He couldn't sleep after he got back into his bed. His anger was making him antsy. Getting up, he went to see what she was doing, hearing her singing to the radio his mom used when she was cooking. "What the hell are you doing? You're trespassing."

"No. You didn't tell me to leave, and you left the door open. That's entering when you're still here. Do you have anything to eat other than three eggs and some dried-up bread?" Going back to his room to get dressed, Del didn't know why, but he thought he'd be able to deal with her better if he was clothed. "You should take a shower while you're at it. You kind of smell like old shoes."

"I fucking hate you." He didn't care if she heard

him. However, he was glad his mom wasn't there. She would have been disappointed in him for saying something like that, even if the woman was irritating him. Going into the bathroom, he thought he did smell, but nothing like old shoes. Turning on the water, he brushed his teeth twice and then stepped into the warm spray.

By the time he was dressed, he could smell something good coming from his kitchen. Del knew how to cook, but he didn't enjoy it as much as his mom did. He also knew how to keep a clean house, which he did every day. But with the woman in the house, he could see where he'd left newspapers out on the coffee table, and his shoes were by the fireplace and not at the front door where they should have been. Entering the kitchen, he was surprised to see the table set for two, as well as glasses of orange juice.

"I found some concentrate in your freezer. There were all kinds of things in there we could eat while you tell me why your company skipped over mine when you were looking for project help." He asked her who the hell she was. "Are you always this snippy in the morning? I know you live here with your mom. The whole town thought you were such a good son for coming home to help her out when she fell. Also, you might find this hard to believe — I know I do — but you're considered a catch by all the single and not so single women in town. A couple of men too, as a matter of fact."

"Your name?" She told him. "All right, Merce Lowery. I'm assuming you have a high-level production company that can take a design and make it a reality."

"Yes. Not only that but we're set up to manufacture the piece in quantity as well as quality." He dug into his omelet and thought she had taken lessons from his mom. It was that good. "You can be nice and say thank you, can't you? I'm sure you have that in your vocabulary someplace."

Instead of doing what she asked, Del asked her for more information about her company. "What's the name of your company, and how long have you been in business?" She answered his questions with a set of her own. He didn't have a problem telling her the same things she was asking him, so they got a lot accomplished in a short amount of time. "Lowery Construction isn't on our list, but perhaps it is because we thought it was just that, a construction company. Being in business for forty years, has anyone ever asked you to build them a home? To put in a driveway or something?"

"Yes to both of those. And we do that when asked. My father, Harlin Lowery, took the business from his father, and that's how they started out. But my dad decided that if we were going to make it in this fast-paced world, we needed to be able to manufacture the things we might need, such as the arm mechanisms you're looking to have made." She pulled out her phone and handed it to him after searching on it. "This is the arm design we did for a car manufacturer in Maine six months ago. The next picture shows a video of our product in use on the line it was designed for. While we did do the work on that and the design, I know your company does all their own specs and measurements for what you need. I was told this piece is for an extra arm in the operating room. To make sure that the patient is being monitored for anesthesia when there isn't enough staff for one reason or another."

"Yes. We're not replacing any of the staff. This will be in use when there isn't anyone to monitor the patient if they're understaffed. It's happened enough that they asked us to come up with a design that could fill in when the need arose." He watched the video twice before handing the phone back to her. "Your design is good, but this is more of a delicate operation. The arm would need to be able to push buttons and sound an alarm when it's needed." Getting up, he brought her his laptop and handed it to her when he found his own mocked-up version of what they were looking for.

"I can see the slick designs on this, as well as the need for it to be all stainless rather than exposed harnessing." She enlarged the photos and looked them over as well. Merce asked him about the design and how it was put together without using things that would attract germs and other items that would cause trouble for an exposed patient. "I can work with this. We have the equipment ready to go with just a few modifications here and there."

"Hold your horses a bit there. We have to interview the others we've already set the appointments with." She nodded, but he could see the disappointment on her face. Del had no idea why, but he didn't like that he'd put it there. "My partner, David, is going to two places tomorrow. Well, today, I guess. And I have one or two today that I'm going to hit up. I like your ability to get things moving, but we need to make this fair across the board. You'll notice that no one else has come pounding on my door at a godawful hour to make me see their specs and ability to get the project going."

"I did notice that. Yes. They must not be as gung ho as I am about things. I'm thinking that should count for something, don't you?" He wasn't sure her upbeat attitude was hiding her real feelings, or she was just like that all the time. He wasn't sure he could handle her being the latter all the time. "Not to mention, I don't believe any of them came by to make you something to eat either."

"It's my food." She shrugged and got up to start clearing the table. "I'll do that. You cooked, and I'll clean. It's the way my mom taught us all how to do it."

"All of you? I'd not heard there were more than you." He told her he had six brothers and a sister. "Your mom must be a saint. To have eight kids around all the time must have been bonkers for anyone. Where were the rest of you when you came home to be with her when she fell? Not to mention, how did she fall? Did you happen to shove her down the stairs or something?"

"I'd not do that to my mom." He looked at her. "Now you? I can see that being tempting where you're concerned. You do make a man wish he'd been smart enough to have run you off when you came around."

"Yeah, I have that happen a great deal." He'd touched a nerve. Her voice and her body stance gave her away. "Anyway, you were going to tell me about the rest of your family."

"My older cousins, really their adopted siblings to us, James, who is married with three kids. They live in Japan right now while he's working. He's been there for about two years now. Mom used to go there to visit, but she said she'd just wait for him to come back home if it came to her seeing him again. My stepsister, Mary, is married too. She has just one child, and he's a little on the rotten side. But then I don't see them much either. The same situation with them as James. She thinks it would be better to wait on them to come back here. They're in Texas living on a ranch of some kind." She asked him about the others. "I'm the youngest of the kids that are my biological brothers. There is Peter, Robert, William—he goes by William, by the way. I can see you calling him Bill to irritate him. Sherman, Darrel—another one that goes by his first name. And then me. Delmar. I was called Del from the first, so there'd be no confusion between me and my granddad. My dad was Del as well, but he passed away before I was born. Grandda is still around but doesn't get out much anymore. He's in his late eighties. Not that he isn't as brilliant as he'd ever been, but he doesn't drive much and won't allow anyone to take time out of their day to go and fetch him, as he calls it. Who do you have in your family?"

"Like you, I'm the youngest. But I only have two brothers, older than me, both married with a family. I'm what one might call a late in life child. My dad was in his late forties when I was born, and my mom, who passed away a few years ago, was in her early forties. Not that she hated me or anything, but it was just too much for her to have a child so late in life, and she ended up in a nursing home when I started grade school." He told her he was sorry. "Me too. I didn't know her, not at all, but I have my brothers, Anthony and Carl, around to tell me things about her. To me, it sounds like she'd been having mental issues before I came along, but I keep that little tidbit to myself. I also have my grandda, who is now in a nursing home, and my dad. Who I love with all that I am."

They talked for a little while longer, and when she yawned, causing him to yawn after her, he told her he needed to take a nap. After she told him she'd be back later to see what he'd been able to figure out, he offered her his mom's room and was surprised when she took him up on it. However, when she was nearly asleep as he told her it was hers to use, Del made his way to his room and turned on his alarm. He still had work to do.

~*~

Merce woke, not knowing for a moment where she was. Stretching when she remembered, she looked around the massive bedroom and wondered at the things that seemed to be sitting on every available space. Getting up, feeling like she'd slept the best sleep she'd ever known, she looked at the pictures scattered around the room like a shotgun blast. Mingled in with the photos, there were things like bottles of sand and a plaster cast of childlike hands. Merce marveled at the things, like a baby blanket behind glass in a frame. There were sad mementos as well as happy ones. A funeral card from what she assumed was Del's father. An obituary cut out from a newspaper that told of the death of three members of a household that died together.

While she had no idea who they were, she knew that it had touched something deep inside of the woman that used this room as her own. Reading it over, Merce put it back just where she found it after reading about the two children and their mother dying from smoke inhalation, then the fire.

Going into the bathroom, she also saw the whimsical part of Mrs. Archer. There were pictures of children in the same bathtub that was in this room. Somehow Merce thought it was Mrs. Archer's own children, taking a bath at the end of a long day of play and adventure.

A beautiful little boy was waving at the camera, his truck taking a bath with him covering his manly parts. Two little boys about the same age were playing with bubbles on their head and chin, just as she'd done a million times when she'd been younger.

The wallpaper was floral, the towel colors an

exact match to it. There were rugs on the floor that she curled her toes into. They were that soft. A shower stall was hidden behind a small door that she fell in love with. Scented soaps and shampoo lined the top. Merce found herself wishing she'd gotten to meet the other woman while she was here. She knew she'd like her. Perhaps if they were to get the project job, she'd get to know the woman a little.

Taking a shower felt wonderful. Washing her hair twice with the herbal shampoo, she made a note of the brand so that she could get herself some. After drying off, she pulled one of the huge thirsty towels around her and stepped back into the bedroom. A woman stood there smiling at her with a piece of luggage in both hands.

"You must be Merce." Merce nodded and told her she was. "I'm Del's mother, Katie Archer. Normally I'd not know who was in the house while I was away, but my son left you a note on the kitchen table. I didn't read it, so if he had any date with you this evening, you'll have to find out from him."

"We're not. Dating, I mean. I came and woke him up in the middle of the night to ask…well, argue with him about why he'd not asked my company to make his design." Her face heated up. "That didn't come out well either."

"I don't imagine it did. I'm sure he didn't take the time to cover himself up either." Again her face heated up, and Merce thought the other woman was enjoying this just a little too much. "Yes, well, I'm going to drop these things off here, and I'll meet you down in the kitchen. I'm going to have to make arrangements with my kids to come and have dinner with me tonight. I've missed them all."

Hurriedly dressing, she made her way downstairs and wondered if the older two were in town. Somehow she didn't think so, or Merce was sure Del would have mentioned it. Stepping into the kitchen again, she was startled by the changes that had only just taken place in the few hours she's been sleeping.

"I have a flower garden and an herb garden out back. When I can, I bring them in the house so I can enjoy their scents. I use them to cook as well, but today they're just for show." Merce asked about the large boxes on the counter. "Oh, those are from Mr. Carder. He's been holding things for me while I was away. Nothing too important like mail, but some of the tomatoes he had in his garden that he made into sauces for me. There is some squash that he put into canning jars as well. I told him we didn't need that much anymore now that my kids are grown, but he insists that I might sometimes, and he makes sure I have them."

There was a basket of eggs—fresh, she'd bet—and apples, as well as smaller baskets of cherries, blackberries, and fruits she didn't know. Picking up a pear, Merce inhaled deeply as she asked if she could have it.

"Oh, of course. I never turn someone away when there are extras around. When you leave here, I'll send a few things home with you. After dinner, of course." Merce asked if she was staying for dinner. "You are. I've spoken to Del, and he said he wanted to speak to you about a couple of things. And the others are coming too. I'll be in heaven."

"Are James and Mary coming as well?" The knife that Katie was using dropped into the sink, and blood dripped from her hand. "You're bleeding. I'm so sorry. I didn't mean to startle you, or whatever I did. Here, let me have a look at it."

Katie allowed her to look at the cut. For whatever reason, she was sure this wasn't her normal way of dealing with a cut. Having her sit down in a chair, Merce held pressure on the wound while Katie spoke. Merce watched the painful emotions as she told her what had happened.

"Several years ago, as if I didn't have the date burned into my heart, I went out to see James. He and

Mary were living in Texas then, and I had gone to visit them. James's wife had just given birth, and I wanted to see their little baby. I was technically his grandma." Merce didn't need to encourage Katie to continue when she paused in her telling. However, it was on her mind that Katie wasn't talking to her so much as she was just letting off a little pain. "James and Mary were my sister's children. The obituary you were reading, that was her. I took them when their father, who had killed the three of them, was taken to prison. They're older than my kids. In fact, I hadn't been married yet, and we had no children. When Del and I had our first boy, the two of them seemed to start growing distant from me. But after a time, they seemed to get over it. Then the others came along. When Del was born, and my husband died, they were nearly out of school. James was living here going to college. Mary was going to a tech school to be a nurse."

"They hurt you, didn't they?" Katie told her it was far worse than that. "I'm so sorry. I've only known you for a few minutes, but I feel like you're the best person to have in someone's corner."

"Thank you, my dear. That was very needed and extremely nice of you. When James had his son, as I said, I went out to see him. I was so excited. My Del, the youngest, had already started college. He was very smart and was taking night classes while finishing high school." She smiled at her. "I'm putting off telling you. I need to, but I don't want to as well. I was there for a day and a half when James told me that he wished to speak to me. Mary came over, and he sent his wife out to do some shopping. I didn't understand. She took the little boy with her when I said I'd watch over him. James told me he didn't want me to have anything to do with him or his family from now on."

"I'm going to hunt him down and tear his dick out, just so you know." Katie laughed, but Merce wasn't kidding. "What was his reason for saying such a thing to you? He'd better have had a damned good one for it."

"He said that when I took them in, it was all right with them to have lived here at first. Since I had no one but them to care for, Mary even agreed that they enjoyed being around me. After I married my Del, James told me it was all right because he had made it so I could devote all my time to them when he was away. Del traveled a great deal as a trucker, and I no longer had to work full time. Neither of us did, in actuality. We only did it because we got to know people around town. Not to mention, it was a nice way to find out what was needed to help out." Katie got up and put a kettle with water in it on the stove as she continued. "Mary said I was selfish to have had other children, that I didn't need them when I had her and her brother. That me not just being their mother was wrong of me, and they wished that instead of their mother dying, it had been me. I didn't know what to say to them. I actually had a moment of fear that they'd killed her after the twins were born. Anyway. They went on about how I had ruined their lives. How I had stolen a good life from them by being a mother to my own children. They didn't care, you see, that my own children were what made me happy. That raising the two of them for my now-dead sister was something I had thought was wonderful as well because they were all the connection I had to her. The two of them wanted things their way, and they were never going to forgive me for doing such a horrid thing as having a family of my own when I should have been there just for them."

"They're little pricks. You know that, don't you?" They both turned when someone spoke from the doorway. It was Del. He agreed with her. "She was hurt by those two, and I'm going to hunt them down and take care of their asses. You want to join me?"

"Yes." Katie hugged her son and then hugged him again as she cried on his shoulder. "I'm so sorry, Mom. I didn't know anything had happened. Do the others know?"

"No. I know I should have told you all, but I was so afraid you'd tell me the same thing." Del asked her if her head had been hurt while she was gone. "No. And I'd appreciate it if you didn't take the tone with me, young man."

"I love you, Mom." She kissed him on the cheek.

When he handed Merce the bags he'd had in his hands, she took them to the counter so she could help out, not sure what she could do, but she felt like an intruder right now.

"Merce, do I have you to thank for this revelation? If I do, then I thank you very much. I think she's been holding it in for some time now."

"Del, leave the girl alone. What did you bring home? Everything I told you?" He said he thought he had, but he kept staring at Merce.

Merce finally turned and looked at him. His mom kept talking about the food in the bag while the two of them stood there. The phone ringing took Katie out of the room, and Del asked her again if she'd done this.

"I only asked her about your stepbrother and sister and if they were coming over when she said she was going to call her kids here." He nodded and laid a file on the table. "I'm sorry, Del. I didn't know there was bad water between them. By the way, I want you to know that I like your mom, and right now, I want to go there and beat the shit out of the two of them. How could they do that to her?"

"I don't know. She's a wonderful person. But it's all right. I think I've known for a while that she was hurting about them. I hadn't noticed the missing cards at her birthday and the holidays until I came here to help her out. And no, I didn't shove her down the stairs." She told him she was sorry about that. "Don't be. I owe you for this. I think she'll be able to talk about it now that the wound is open. I really am grateful to you for having her talk about it."

Merce hadn't really done anything but talk to the other woman. And she really did like her. But those others, her stepchildren, needed to have their heads knocked around. Not a little bit either. She was beginning to like her grandda's saying of sparing the rod would spoil the children. Their parents must have been real wieners.

Chapter 2

It was nice having her sons home for a while. They'd all brought her something too. Chocolates and roses. Plants she could put into her garden, as well as a few heirloom seeds they'd gotten off the Internet. Katie loved every one of the gifts, but her sons most of all. They were still waiting on Peter. He'd called and said he was picking something up. She wished they'd not gone to the trouble but was happy they cared enough.

"I'm here." She went to the front door to scold her oldest when she saw what he'd picked up for her. There, standing in the flesh, was Delmar, her father-in-law. "I called him and told him to be ready to come out with me. I had no idea that he'd be packed up and ready to leave that place when I got there."

"Delmar Archer, you've finally come to your

senses? Are you finally going to be among the living again?" He said he would if she'd have him. "Of course, you old buzzard. I have been wanting to have you here for a long time. Come into the kitchen. You know that's the meeting place."

Katie made her way to the bathroom to gather her emotions around her. Delmar had been her saving grace for many years after her husband had passed away. Now with him feeling his age, what he'd told Peter on the way over, she wanted to help him. The knock at the door startled her. Opening it up, she wasn't surprised to see Merce there looking concerned.

"Are you all right? Do you want me to beat someone up for you?" Merce was a breath of fresh air to her. Katie told her that her heart was taking a beating today. "Well, I would imagine it would be. Your father-in-law, Del introduced us to each other when you left, told me he thinks I'm a pretty little thing." Merce snorted. "I can bench press a hundred and twenty pounds. I'm six foot one. I think I've not been called little since I was little. Are you really all right?"

"I am. I thought you were tall. My goodness. I believe all my sons are only a couple of inches taller than you are." When Merce looked in the room where they were all standing, Katie noticed she only had eyes for Del. "Did he give you the project?"

"No. But he said he has a story to tell us at the table. Is that normal for these guys? To vent at the table? When I was little — there's that word again — my brothers would vent too, but usually to me. They thought that since I was so much younger than them, I needed them to boss me around. I fixed that." Katie hugged her. "You're a nice lady, Mrs. Archer. I do hope you get the opportunity to make sure those other two get their heads out of their asses soon enough."

"I do as well. And please call me Katie. There is more to this trouble with them than I told you and Del, but it's all right now. Getting that off my chest and having Delmar here is making everything seem less stressful." Merce told her that the guys were ready with dinner if she was. "I am. And I'm so happy you're staying. It'll be nice to have another woman at the table with me."

"I'm not sure how much I'll be helpful to you. I'm not what a person might call a girly kind of girl. I'm more of a spit in their eye sort of person." Katie told her she'd gotten that. "I thought you might have. Del is a nice man. Everyone I've met so far is. Why hasn't anyone snatched them up? If you don't mind me asking."

"Not at all. I think it has more to do with the

fact that they've been working on getting themselves established. Come on, Merce. Let's go and let me brag on my children for a few minutes." She asked her if she knew they were grown men. "Not to me. Not ever."

The table was set, and she was happy to see they'd put the flowers they'd gotten her in vases on the table and around the room. The chocolates were on her candy tray that had been her mother's. She couldn't remember the last time she'd used this room. It had only been her and Del for a while now, and they usually ate in the kitchen.

After they filled their plates with the side dishes, Peter and Del brought in the steaks and chicken. She didn't care for red meat, and they always made sure she had something to eat with them. Katie noticed that Merce didn't take a steak either. But her potato was piled high with sour cream, chives, bacon bits, as well as cheese. However, Katie saw that she skipped over the salad.

"You had something to tell us." Peter put some salad in a small bowl and set it in front of Merce as he spoke to Del. She promptly smacked his hand and put it back in the large bowl. "You need some greens to go with your dinner."

"But Daddy, I had a salad last month. Doesn't that count?" Everyone laughed, and Peter's face turned a bright red. "I'm a grown assed woman, Peter. Leave me to my own eating habits, and I'll leave your namesake where it is. Right between your legs."

There hadn't been this much laughter in their home for a while, Katie realized. The last time the boys had been home all together was last Christmas. And they'd been so busy it had been just the single day with them before they were running off again. This was, she thought, the best time she'd had in a long time. Even Delmar was laughing at the antics going on. Peter reminded his brother again of his story.

"Yes, all right. I had some appointments today to find out if there was someone local that could do this project for the new equipment we're manufacturing. The first one I went to, the owner met me at the door. He wouldn't even let me in." Merce asked him if it was Mr. Donaldson. "Yes, that's right. Do you know him?"

"Sort of. He's an ass and thinks if he doesn't make whatever is being made, it isn't worth his time to get it put together. If you'd like, you can run the other names by me, and I can perhaps help you out. I won't down mouth them, I promise. But I will be honest about their work." Del thanked her and then glanced at her. Smiling at her youngest son, he smiled back. "There are three other people that can do the work but won't. Capital is the biggest thing. But back to Mr.

Donaldson. What did he tell you?"

"Just what you said. That he didn't come up with the design, and he didn't think—no, he said he didn't work on subpar designs that would have his name on them. Then he proceeded to walk me back to my car. What a jerk." Robert asked him about the job. Del explained it to his brothers as they ate their dinner. "After I left his plant, I called it into the office and had him investigated, just to be sure he wasn't having other troubles. He is. Big time. This project would have gotten him out of the hole, but turning it down because he'd not designed it is going to put him under, I'm betting."

"My dad will more than likely end up purchasing the company. He's really good at that sort of thing. Buying up failing companies, then making them viable again. I should have mentioned to you earlier that Lowery Construction also owns Arts Designs, as well as Shepherds Works. They don't do what you need, but they are very good at working around designs for logos as well as advertising." Everyone at the table turned to Merce. "What? You can't tell me you don't branch out on other things as well. I mean, how do you think we're able to afford to get the equipment we need to make designs like you might need in the future?"

"For the most part, we're attorneys. Darrel is a

doctor. And Del is a designer for equipment he sees a need for." She asked William if he liked his job. "What do you mean? Like being an attorney? It's good pay, and I'm good at it. We're partners in our own law firm."

"But do you like it? Do you enjoy being an attorney? I really like what I do. So does my dad. We not only have several companies we work with to become viable again, but we also work with other companies that might need a hand-up once in a while. It's fun giving back when we can." Merce looked around the table. "Do you like being attorneys? Or doctors? I know Del loves his job. He shows it when he talks about it. But you guys, you just seem to have jobs that pay well."

Katie watched her sons as they seemed to struggle with her question. She'd not thought they went to college to be attorneys for any reason other than that was something they wanted to do. But the looks on their faces told her they'd done just what Merce had pointed out to them—gone after their jobs because they paid well.

"You know what, I don't care for it." When Sherman said that, he smiled at Merce. "I've been thinking along the lines that since I have the education, I have money in the bank, and I'm good at it, I should keep at it. But I don't like it like I think I should."

"I do love it," Robert spoke up, then shook his head. "No, that's not true. I used to love it. I used to look forward to going to the courtroom and making sure my client got the best deal. But they're all shitheads for the most part. What I'd really like to do is teach law. Be the person that can tell them exactly what to expect in the courtroom, not what it says in the books we got. To be able to tell them things you have to learn on your own. Such as, you study for years to become the best you can be, and all you have to show for it is a lot of debt when you get out and no place to hang your name. I was lucky in that my brothers and I decided to be together right from the start as a firm. But that wasn't the right way to go either, I'm thinking. We have everything in common, but nothing to talk about but some dick we got off only to see him in the courtroom a few weeks later for the same thing."

They talked over one another about how much they didn't enjoy what they did. It was an eye-opener for Katie to see that they'd only done what they did for the money. As it turned out, the only one that seemed to enjoy being an attorney that he had gone to college for was Peter. But he only enjoyed the pro-bono stuff rather than going to court, as his brothers had pointed out, for shit heads.

"I used to love what I did for fun after retirement."

Merce asked Delmar what it was he'd done. "Believe it or not, I was a gardener. We didn't need to work for the money after I retired from working as a county clerk for the tax department. So I started out by plowing up gardens around the neighborhood. Sometimes people having themselves a little plot of food growing was the difference between starving and having a good meal. But I began to branch out. Putting in larger gardens that would have trees and flowers and such. I think my old greenhouse is still on the property we used to live on."

"My grandda used to plant flowers around the neighborhood when he was retired too. Nothing fancy, but he would load up his old beater of a truck and go around and plant flowers around the town. I think the courthouse was his biggest project, and he so loved having the pretty blooms to show off." Delmar said he remembered him. "He might well remember you too if you were in the courthouse when he was around. He's not doing well now. I think his heart just broke when my grandma died some years ago. I've been telling my brothers that he needs to get out of that place and live, but I don't have any kind of power to do it."

"Why not?" Merce told Peter that her brothers had power of attorney over him since he'd moved into the place. "You need to kidnap him for a few hours daily. I can arrange that if you want. I think it would be fun to have him and Grandda tooling around and planting flowers and planning trouble. You can do that for him as his granddaughter."

"Really? I'd love that. I know my dad would too. He goes to see him once a day, and I think having him at home would do both of them a world of good. Thank you, Peter. If you can arrange that, I'd be forever grateful to you." He said he'd work on it tomorrow. "Thanks."

She told him where he was and his full name. Delmar perked up when Merce said him coming home would be so much fun. Not only did he know the other man, but he had had lunch with him a few times in the past and had enjoyed his banter and laughter at the silliest things. Katie was glad to see that Delmar was looking forward to something after being stuck in a nursing home for so long. And even though he put himself in there, he'd wanted out in the worst kind of way, he'd told her as her sons talked about what they really wanted to do.

As soon as dinner was over and desserts were passed around, she sat and listened to her sons talking about their lives. Katie had only been gone for a few months on the cruise ship, but it seemed as if she'd missed so much. She thought perhaps she'd missed a great deal even before she'd left home to have what she had hoped was fun. Then Merce turned to her and told her she needed to talk to her sons.

"You, my dear, are too pushy." Katie smiled. And instead of taking offense, Merce told her she needed her around. "I do believe I do. You've been here one day, and I feel like I need you around forever. We're having such a good time. I'm not sure I want to tell them the rest. By the way, how did you find out?"

"I didn't until you just told me. You were fired — or did you quit?" She said they fired her. "I'm assuming they thought they had good reason. All Del and the others have talked about is what a good cook you are. So that can't be it."

"It was, actually. I was cooking things I thought everyone would enjoy. And they did, more than they did the other food places on the ship. The buffet is a high-profit margin for them, and I was taking people away from that and having them go to the restaurant I was in charge of." Merce said that was just stupid. "I thought so as well. But they paid me severance pay and gave me a ticket home. I'm glad, in a way. I think I needed to be here more than seeing if I could have fun on a cruise. Which I have to admit, I didn't."

"Good for you."

The two of them talked well after the dishes were

cleaned up, and they all retired to the living room. Merce received two calls, which she didn't talk about. The girl looked upset, and as much as she wanted to ask her about it, Katie didn't know that she wanted her to tell her just yet. They were, as she said before, having a nice evening.

~*~

Del explained to Merce and her dad what he needed. Then, after a tour of their plant, he was sure that she and her company were the best fit. While standing there watching the machinery work on part of what he'd wanted, he looked around the place and was impressed by not just what he saw in equipment but how the employees seemed to take pride in what they were doing. It was, in a weird sort of way, a happy place.

"Are you with us now, Del?" He grinned at Harlin, what he'd been asked to call the older man. "You seemed to have spaced out there a little. Merce stomped off when she couldn't get your attention. But then she's usually upset about one thing or another of late."

"She's brilliant, in the event you weren't aware of that." Harlin nodded as he moved around with him. "This place, it's the right fit for what we need. I'm thinking we can use you and your company for a lot of the projects we have going right now."

"Did Merce tell you she has two older brothers?" Del nodded, not sure where that had come from. "Let me get to that. I can see on your face that you're slightly confused at my statement. But her brothers, Harley and Brock, are quite a few years older than she is. Ten and twelve years, as a matter of fact. You should, if you meet them, tell them how brilliant their little sister is. Harley, he still thinks she's ten or so and needs to have someone check her checking account now and again. He doesn't anymore. She put her foot through his ass when he tried it, but it's not to say they don't treat her as a child."

"I'm betting that's not all that she did to them." Harlin laughed and said it wasn't. "I like her boldness. However, I do worry about her. She got a couple of calls yesterday at my house that I think upset her. My mom was the most worried. She also took to liking her very much. We didn't ask, but I'm not sure it was good news."

"She didn't mention it. I'll see what I can find out. We have a good relationship, she and I. However, she's much closer to my dad. I'm to understand she is going to kidnap him a few hours a day when she can. I'm not going to mention it to her brothers. They'll think she's not old enough to handle him. Not that he's a handful, but they think someone in their eighties needs constant care."

"My grandfather is the same age. If they were to say something like that to him, he'd shove his boot up their asses too." They were laughing as they came around to find Merce again. She looked upset again, and a part of Del wanted to slay the dragon for her. When her dad asked her what was wrong, she blew up.

"Harley said I need to make sure I'm not spending the night with any random man I come across. If that wasn't bad enough, he asked me if I had thought about getting on birth control if I was going to be promiscuous. Mother fucker. After I hung up on him, Brock called me to ask if I needed him to find me a good doctor to get me on some kind of birth control. Like I'm a fucking idiot. I tell you, Dad, if they were here right now, I'd show them a thing or two." Del was so shocked when Harlin laughed that he could only stare at the man. "You think this is funny, Dad? They're treating me like I'm a whore or something. I didn't sleep with Del. I stayed there because it was better than me driving home exhausted. And even if I did want to fuck him, it's none of their damned business."

"No, it's not. I'm not laughing at you, honey, but I was thinking about what had gotten into their head to think to say something like that to you. And what you said back to them."

Harlin was still laughing as he told her he'd call them and give them a piece of his mind. He was still laughing when Del saw the man picking up his phone in his office. Del looked at Merce.

"Are you pissed?" Del asked her why she thought he'd be pissed. "I don't know. Basically, they called you a bastard for leading me astray."

"Would you mind very much if I were to talk to them?" He smiled at her. "I'm not sure there would be a great deal of talking. I tend to get someone's attention first with my fists. Then after that, they get it in their head that I'm not a pushover."

"You'd hit them for me?" Del said he was sure she could take care of herself. "I can, but it's nice to know you're not going to be letting them get by with this shit either. Sometimes I don't like them at all. I love them dearly, but I don't have to like them."

"No, you don't. But if you tell me where they are right now, I'll go over and straighten them out. I might even take my mom with me. She'd surely defend your honor a good deal better than I might." Merce asked him if he was serious. "I am if you want me to be. Mom really likes you, and it would bother her to no end to find out that someone said those things to you.

But if I were you, when my mom goes there, I'd go with her. She can be very vocal when she's pissed off at someone."

"If you're serious, I'm going to call her right now. Tell her exactly what they said to me." Del told her to go for it. "Thanks. I'm going to."

When she walked away, pulling out her phone, Del was left in the plant alone. Walking around, getting another feel for the place, he noticed little things he'd not before. It made him smile to know that this company took care of their employees as he did, even though they were in a large factory.

There were pictures of families in their workstations. Someone had hung up a copy of a report card, and it had hearts all around it. Baby pictures, too, along with family vacations. Taking a closer look, he could see Merce in a few. Harlin as well. They did take working for a family to the highest marks.

"Your mom is going with me. She said for you to come along as well. Do you mind?" He didn't and told her that. "Great. Maybe she can knock some sense into their heads. I haven't been able to. Dad is talking to them now, and I doubt it will make a difference."

Looking forward to this more than he thought he should have, Harlin said he'd come along too. He wanted to see someone else take action. As soon as they were inside the building, Merce was greeted with hugs and questions on how she was doing. If nothing else, the staff at her brothers' firm seemed to like her.

The brothers were partners in a real estate office. Lowery Brothers — he thought it a silly name — had trophies all over the room about their sales meeting huge goals, as well as letters from families that had used them to purchase a home. He wondered if any of them knew how they treated their sister.

"Yes, I'd like to speak to Harley and Brock Lowery, please." His mom smiled at the woman who sat at the front desk. "Tell them it's Katherine Archer. That should get them moving."

Few people knew their mother as Katherine Archer. He was sure that about half the county thought she was just Katie Archer, mother to six boys and a good soul. But his mother was so much more than that. Katherine Archer was a multi-billionaire. A tycoon. One who could turn a dime into a million in very little time. Her name opened doors and slammed them shut when she wanted. His mom didn't use her power much, but when she did, people sat up and took notice.

His parents had not always been wealthy. Mom and dad both had invested well and often. Mom had the touch, Del had always thought. When she saw something that piqued her interest, she would research it then invest. Heavily. Sometimes even buying the company to have a good idea where it was going. Del had too been able to know when to buy and sell as well. It helped his company ventures very nicely.

Apparently, the brothers Lowery had heard of her as well. Not only were they shown into a lovely room, but they were offered drinks, snacks, as well as asked if the air conditioning was the right temperature. The staff was falling all over themselves, trying to make sure this woman was as happy as she could be. So, in turn, they were as well.

"Dad? Merce? I didn't know you were in here. I'll have you moved to one of the offices." Mom told the man to sit down and shut up. He did. So did his brother when he walked into the room, wondering why his dad and sister were there. "I'm sorry, Mrs. Archer. I didn't know they were in here when we had our staff make sure you were comfortable."

"So had it been only them and not my son and I, you'd have not cared if they were comfortable?" Both men looked at their dad when Mom spoke to them. "Don't look at him for support, you dimwitted morons. They're with me. I'm here to talk to you about how you've been treating Ms. Lowery here."

"I'm not sure what you mean." Blue tie brother

looked at Merce. "Have you been spreading stories again, Merce? You know it's not right to do that. Do we have to have a talk — ?"

"Oh, for the love of shit. Do you forever talk to her that way? Or is it every woman? No wonder you're still single men." Mom looked at Del. "Darling, I'd like you to take notes on this. Not to treat every woman like a bimbo. Tell your brothers that as well."

"We'd never do that to anyone." Del asked them if they only did it to their sister. "You don't know what it's been for us to be responsible for her. She's only a child."

"I don't know if you've not noticed this or not, but she's far from a child. She's a grown woman. The last time I looked, anyone over the age of twenty-one is old enough to no longer have anyone responsible for them." Mom turned and looked at Harlin. "When was the last time you had to have a talk to your daughter about her behavior, Harlin? I'm betting it's been a while."

"Not since she was about ten. She's always had a good head on her shoulders." He looked at his sons. "Perhaps you can tell me why you think it is that I'm not taking care of Merce. Or tell me a time or two when you've had to bail her out."

"It's because we keep a close eye on her, that's

why." Del stood up and smiled at the two men when
they looked at him. He did notice that neither of them
stood up after glancing at his mom. "Do you have
something to add, Mr. Archer? I'm sure if you've spent
any time with our sister, you can tell your mother we're
right in how we've been caring for her."

    "How old are you two anyway?" They told him
they were in their late thirties. "Late thirties, huh? I
would have thought you were born back in prehistoric
times the way you talk about taking care of Merce.
Were you aware that she has a college degree? That
she helps your father run the business that kept you
clothed, food on your table, as well as money in your
pockets when you were younger than her? Also, you
might find this hard to believe, but she's smart. A go-
getter when it comes to bringing in more business.
Have you been to the plant lately? I noticed things
today that might surprise you. There are pictures on
the walls around the people that work for them of their
families. Your father and sister are in a great many of
the photos, having a good time with the people that
work for them. When was the last time you had a
company outing? That you let your employees put
a little plant or a picture of their own family on their
desk? I'm observant, gentlemen, and I'm thinking that
given a choice, they'd rather work for your sister than

the two of you."

"What does any of this have to do with the two of you coming in here with our little sister?" Del asked the man to stand up, then asked him his name. "I'm Harley Lowery. This is my brother Brock. If you have nothing positive to add to the conversation we were having with your mother, Del, then I'd like you to wait outside with my family."

The punch to his face was satisfactory. Not only that, but he found that he wanted to pick the man up and hit him again. He might well have had his mother not told him to stop. Harley didn't move but asked him what that was for. Del noticed that Brock didn't move so much as his feet out of his way when Harley reached for his sibling.

"That's for thinking I wasn't a gentleman when your sister stayed at my home. I shouldn't have to explain to you that rather than driving home exhausted and risking an accident, she opted to stay in my home in my mom's room. Not for driving too fast or for being on a drunken binge. Nor for being...." He looked at Merce. "What is it they said you were doing?"

"'Fucking around with strangers.'" She kicked her brother in the ribs while he was still down. Del pulled her into his body so she'd not cause him more harm. It was like holding onto a live wire. "You fucking bastard. I've never had sex, much less with random men. You might well have known that about me if you'd get your heads out of your asses and talk *to* me instead of *at* me."

Mom stood up then, as did the men. "If I had a piece of anything to sell, I'd not use you. That's not written in stone, but as far as I can see, it might as well be. Imagine treating your own sister like she was some sort of tramp…. Well, you can bet I'll be bringing this up at my next board meeting." She started away, then turned back to them. "This isn't a way to get you to treat this wonderful young woman better. This is a way for you to think about your actions before it's too late. Let me ask you something while I'm thinking on it. When was the last time you visited your grandfather? Or your father, for that matter. You know, before you know it, they'll be gone, then there won't be any time for them. I lost my husband, a dear and wonderful person, one day because he'd gone to bed and never woke up. He was young too, in his late forties. Just like that, I was a widow with six sons to raise. But the time we had together was wonderful. I'd not miss any of it if I had it all to do it over again. What are you going to think about when not only is your grandfather gone from this earth, but your father as well?"

Mom asked if they could go to dinner when they

were in the car. Del told her he'd love that, and Harlin asked if his father could join them. Stopping by the nursing home, Mom and Merce went into the place to get him. Harlin turned to him when they were gone.

"They won't change. I don't think I thought about how seriously messed up they are about Merce until I saw it through yours and your mother's eyes. I have no idea how they got to this point either. I certainly never treated her that way." Del asked about his wife. "She was gone before Merce was very old. I don't think she was overprotective as much as they are to their sister, but she did have trouble with them leaving the house and letting them play with other children. Do you think they got that from her? I don't mean her ways, but that they had to be the protector because their mother wasn't there to do it?"

"I don't know. I mean, if you think about it, it does make perfect sense." Harlin said he thought so as well. "Harlin, would you mind very much if I started seeing your daughter? I'm not really asking for permission here, but I am asking if you think her brothers will say something to her. Or even hurt her in some way."

"Son, I have to tell you something. When I met you, I thought you were a perfect match for her. I nearly wet myself when you hit her brother. However,

I will tell you I didn't have any idea that you were *the* Archers." Del told him that they were just the Archers. "To you perhaps, but when I saw my sons falling over themselves to please your mother, I did a little looking around on the Internet while my sons were getting their asses handed to him. I don't know if you realize this or not, but your family really are *the* Archers, son. You're richer than Midas, as my dad used to tell people about us. Yes, it would do me a world of good to see the two of you dating. I think she'd enjoy herself too."

Del wasn't sure why he'd asked. He wasn't even sure when he'd realized he wanted to start seeing Merce. But he did. He wanted to see her all dressed up in a pretty dress and having him hanging on her arm. Del would never presume to think she would be on his arm unless she wanted to be there. Laughing, he was thrilled to death to see his mom talking to the elder Lowery. And he seemed to be enjoying himself too.

Chapter 3

Merce watched the prototype arm as it moved through the motions. It was being recorded, too, something they'd only just started doing since taking on this project. She wanted to be able to go over the way it moved with Del, and since he was out of town for a few days, Merce thought this was the best way for them to do it.

"I don't like the way it moves." Not looking at Billy, she asked him why not. What did he see? "It's clumsy. Like it knows what it's supposed to be doing, but it has to think about it too long. Like a person that has only just gotten a body, and they're learning how to walk. They don't want to mess up."

"Maybe that's what he wants. I mean, this isn't like an arm putting a door on a car. This is going to be for an operating room where lives are at stake." He asked her if he could tweak the program a little. "Just don't save it over theirs. I don't want them coming back on us and telling us we fucked them over."

Not that she thought they would do that. David had spent the entire day yesterday at their plant just looking around with her. He had pointed out the things that Del had told him about. The way the workers were happy, and the number of personal things they had around them. He even went over the design with her, telling her that if after producing one of them they found errors, not to hesitate to work on them. They were perhaps the best company they'd worked with.

While Billy worked on his tweaking job, she went back to her office. She didn't have anything in her office to say that she was the one working out of it. There were no family pictures around. Not a single piece of art. There were no little things she'd picked up on vacation. Merce hadn't been on vacation since… well, she didn't remember the last time.

Moving to the busy side of her desk, she sat down and closed her eyes. Merce had been working almost nonstop on this project for five days now. She'd even slept here last night in order to be here bright and early for the first finished prototype. As she sat there resting, she thought of Del.

He'd asked her out when they'd spoken on the phone yesterday. Merce had hesitated long enough for him to change the subject. What she'd been thinking about was how long it had been since the last time she'd been out on a date, even with her dad. She needed to do that more too. Have some fun with her dad and grandda.

Merce did have a date with her grandda tonight. They were going to get some dinner, just the two of them, then head back to her apartment to play some chess. The other day when they'd been out, he'd told her how much he missed the game. Telling him she'd get them a set had tickled them both. She was glad now that she'd been able to find them a good set for them to play with. However, she was much more excited to have Del ask her out again. This time she'd be ready for it.

"I have a couple of questions for you. Well, I don't, but David does. He's on line two." She punched in the number and put it on speaker phone. Her dad, always thinking no one could hear him on speaker phone, yelled at David that she was here. "Go ahead, ask her what you were asking me."

A short burst of laughter from David had her smiling. "The first hospital we're making this for just called. They want to know how hard it would be to put a permanent sign on the machines telling how to use it." Merce asked him why they'd want to do that. "I would imagine so that there isn't any confusion on how it works."

"No, what I mean is, why do they want it to be permanent? It wouldn't be any trouble to have it put into the stainless steel before it's put together, but what if there are upgrades to it? You do want it so it's easy to upgrade, correct?" He said he'd not thought of that. "I have put that in the design. A way it can be worked on without taking it apart too much. But the user information we'd put on there would be outdated the first time we had to do that sort of updates on it."

"That's a good point. I wonder if Del had thought of that." She could have told him it wasn't on the specs but didn't. "There are a couple of other things they want on it. I'm not entirely sure how I feel about this part. They want their name on it—Jackson Memorial Hospital. We will have both our names on it, as well as the manufacturer and design companies, but adding their hospital name seems like it would lessen the resale value but increase their cost to purchase it. It seems silly to me when it's in their hospital."

"Maybe that's why. They want to have it known that it was made for them especially. It's a vanity thing. And I have no idea how much you'd charge for that sort of input, but again, that would be easy to put on there for them." David asked her if they had run into this sort of thing before. "You mean the vanity thing? Yes. Quite a bit, as a matter of fact. A couple of years ago, this company wanted their opening date put on the machine they wanted. Within two years, they were out of business. Not that I'm saying this will happen to the hospital, but I just read an article the other day about two hospitals being combined into one, and the other one was renamed. If that were to happen, they'd have a piece of equipment with a name of a hospital on it that no longer existed. I would imagine people would then think they're using old, outdated equipment."

"What a brilliant argument. Would you mind if I pitched that to them? Not the selling part, but that the equipment would seem outdated to people that might need it. Brilliant. No wonder Del endlessly talks about how smart you are." She looked at her dad, and he winked at her. "All right. You've given me a great deal of information. I'm so glad I called. Thank you so much."

When the call was disconnected, she looked at her dad. "You could have told him that same information. Why did you come to me for it?" He looked guilty, and she asked him again. "Tell me, Dad. What's going on?"

"I'm wanting to retire." She sat back in her chair.

This was news to her. "I've been thinking about it for a few weeks now. But lately, hanging out with my dad has been so much fun I no longer want to go to work and have to take him back to the nursing home. I think he's enjoying it as well."

"I know he is. It's all he talks about when I hang out with him." Dad nodded. "Will you take him home with you for good? I wonder what your sons will have to say to that."

"They're no longer your brothers?" Dad laughed and said he didn't blame her. "I don't care. After last week with them, I'm having a hard time thinking of them in a nice way too. But yes, I'd take him home with me. Perhaps if it got too bad for him, I'd just hire someone to come in and help out. But I think he's more energetic. I know he's eating more. Just the other day, he was telling me that he had two bowls of oats for breakfast."

"I don't know why anyone would want just one of them. But I do understand. We're having dinner tonight. I have a feeling he's going to ask if he can not go back. I didn't tell him about the fight I had with Harley and Brock, but he told me that he gets lonely with no one around to see him very much. I don't know why, but I thought they'd be seeing him all the time to make sure that he's in compliance with what they think he should be doing." Dad told her that she was right in thinking that. He had as well. "If retiring is what you want to do, then I'd say go for it. So long as you let me know who you're going to have run this place. I don't want to be blindsided by someone I can't work with."

"What do you mean?" She said he'd have to leave someone in charge while he was retired. She wanted to know if he had a list of names yet. "Honey, there is only one person I'd leave this place for, and that would be you. You might not realize this, but you've been running it for a long time. I've just been showing up to hang out with you."

"Dad, that's not true. You're a vital part of this company." He nodded and said he might well be, but she still ran it. "I don't know about that, but I do love working here. And the people. Are you sure you want to leave it to me? I mean, I'm very promiscuous and still basically a child."

"Yes, I've noticed that about you too." Dad stood up. "The paperwork is at the attorney's office now. As I said, I've been thinking about this for a while now, and I think you're going to make this business better than it's ever been. My dad agrees with me. He said you'd make it shine. Whatever that means to an eighty-year-old man."

She was still sitting at her desk when her phone rang. Picking it up, she said the name of the company and waited for someone to speak on the other end of the phone. Nearly ready to hang up, she heard Del speaking to someone that was apparently with him.

"Del?" He asked her to hang on a second. She could tell he was angry and didn't make any snide comments as she usually did. When he asked her if he could call her back, she said it was all right. "Is everything all right there? Do I need to come there and bail you out?"

"Maybe. But I will call you back. Will you have dinner with me tomorrow night?" She told him she would. "Good. That makes me feel better already. I'll call you right back."

It had never been anything she'd done before, worrying about another person. She didn't count her dad or grandda — they were family. But with Del, it really made her feel like she really needed to drop everything and run to his side. It was the strangest feeling she'd ever had.

When her phone rang again, she picked it up, saying his name. His laughter made her feel better, but she was no less worried about him. Asking him what was going on, she heard someone, although muffled, talking in the background.

"I'm in Arizona with this company that wants us to retool their entire line for what it cost them to have the outdated lines put in the building when it was built nine years ago. Not only that, but this owner thinks we should feel privileged for doing this for them, as they are number two—not one, but two—in the market for getting their product out on time." She asked him what they did. "They're a warehouse that sends items to places like dollar stores all over this side of the country. I think he said something like four-thousand stores. I quit listening to him when he called me a dummy. Whatever. So now I've locked myself in his office so I could pretend to talk to someone with higher authority than me. He wants me to see, whoever my boss might be, if they're willing to take a huge cut in profit, not to mention time and energy since he wants it done in two weeks."

"I'm used to clients like him. Tell me the specs you would need to make this work for them, and I'll be your higher authority. I think him thinking you have a female for a boss would make his nuts curl up around his tonsils." Laughing, Del told her what he'd told the other man. "I'm assuming he wants more than one of the door readers. And this price you quoted him, it's a little on the lower side?"

"Yes. If we were doing all twenty-eight of his bay

doors, it would cost less. It would just be a repetitive job by then. But the one he wants for the system at the higher level, outside of the mods, he called them, that's going to be costly. There are three levels per mod, and he had fifty mods." She asked him if they used conveyor belts with wheels and rubber treads. "They do, as a matter of fact. Why? Do you know something I don't?"

"I doubt that. But if they're using conveyors to put their things on the trucks, it would be helpful for me to know if they have roll-tainers. I think they call them on that level. These would be loaded up for each store and then rolled into the stores per department. That would mean you'd have to have a program for each store and what they consider each department. Such as, health and beauty aids might not include things like headbands for children. You'd need to put that into each store's inventory. Or make them all the same. Which is costly at the other end, and not usually something a store might be willing to pay for simply because the warehouse is changing their way of doing things." Del asked her how she knew this. "When I have to go into a warehouse, which is more often than not, I have to know exactly what they might want and how they might think things need to be distributed. I try hard to be able to work with each department to know what it is they do. I've found out that just because a person is in charge of a certain area, they might not know squat about how it's really run. What they think is needed and what is actually needed are two very different things."

When she was ready to speak to the company manager, Del stayed on the open line with her. She wanted him there, but he also thought he could learn a little more if he heard this man's ideas. As soon as Markus said hello after introducing the two of them, Merce started talking like she'd been working with him since the beginning. Del was so impressed, he called David and let him listen in on the conversations too.

"So, as you can understand, there isn't going to be just a simple fix for your warehouse, Markus. As soon as we start moving departments around and having the labels redesigned, things are going to go from bad to worse for you and your company." Markus asked her how they could go at this cheaper. "Cheaper? Well, I would say that you need to start from the beginning. Such as, you leave the building up that you are using now and work with our company in getting the most up-to-date equipment and programs into place. While that is being worked over, let your stores know you're improving for their benefit. And it will be once you're finished. The stores could download a copy of every item they ordered and be able to compare it to the list they'll get when the truck is unloaded. New belts in the new warehouse will last longer, as well as not slide and tangle up with the product going down the line. There are other advantages too that you might not be aware of. If you hire more employees than you currently have, the government might be so thrilled with you that they give you a low-interest or even a no-interest loan on the construction. That right there will save you millions of dollars. Then, once you get the new warehouse set up, you have yourself an entire building for extra product, as well as overstocks that you can't carry now. I think everyone can be happy with that."

"Why didn't this other fella tell me all this?" Del was worried for a moment, but he knew he shouldn't have been when she answered Markus. "I suppose I did put a lot of demands on him without listening to what he was talking to me about. Yes, I can see where I messed up with this. But this is a great deal of money."

"Yes, it is. It is also a great deal more income for you and your partners if you have any." He said he was the sole owner. "Great. There is no long, drawn-out committee that you have to wait months on to get their heads out of their asses—you'll be able to make decisions on your own. Del is the man to go to when you want the best. The company is one that doesn't cut corners and will give you the best value for what you want. If you wish to go ahead and get things done the way you wanted, I'm afraid there isn't any way that we can help you. You'll—"

"No, no. I think you're right. I have to expand and get this place up to date. I will admit, I'm spending more money on repairs than I care to. What sort of guarantee do you think I can get on this upgrade and new system?" She told him that wasn't her department, that she was more of the hit you between the eyes sort of person. "You have that down very well, honey. You would make a great politician. Someone that doesn't hold back. I'm going to stop talking and listen to what Del here has to say to me. You should have come with him. I'd love to have had dinner with you."

"Markus, I'm not the boss of Del. I'm just a woman that can be calm when it's necessary and a bitch when that's needed too." He asked her what she thought he was, and Del closed his eyes, waiting for Merce to answer him.

"I thought I was going to have to go there and kick your ass to see reason. Then after talking to you for a few minutes, I changed that to a middle ground. By the end, you impressed me with being a calm man. You should make a habit of listening to people who know a bit more than you do about things. I'm sure that if asked, Del wouldn't know nearly as much as you do about running a warehouse. However, he can and will walk circles around you when it comes to putting the right equipment in the right place to create a good workplace."

For the next several hours, the three of them—David, Del, and Markus—talked about what would be needed for the upgrade. Del was impressed that he was pretty much leaving the programing and equipment up to him and David. Also that he seemed a good deal more excited about the upgrades than he had been for the repair work Del had been called out here for.

Once he was in his car, David called him back and asked him to call Merce. As soon as she answered, Del told her he loved her for what she'd been able to do for him. Then he told her how she'd sealed the deal for them and that they would be able to hire more people to work on this project, even to expand. When she thanked him, he knew immediately that something had happened. He asked her about it.

"Not now. I'll see you tomorrow night, right?" Del told her he would. "Then I'll talk to you then. I might even need a few hugs."

"It would be my pleasure."

Del was able to get her out of her slump and had

her laughing. She was so excited for them. When they finally hung up the connections, Del decided he was going to finish up as soon as he could and fly back home. He needed to see her as much as she did him.

~*~

Harley put the phone back in the cradle and sat there with his hands holding his head up. This was a nightmare. They were so fucked right now, he wasn't sure what they could do about working this out, so they came out on top. Calling Brock to come into his office, he told him to close the door. As soon as he sat down, Harley told him what was going on.

"I don't understand. Why would they sell this building without giving us first dibs on it? That's very unprofessional of them." Harley just stared at his brother. "We have a twenty-year lease with this building. I'm sure we have a few more years left on it."

"No, we have ninety days. Thirty more than we should be getting. The new owners had it put in the sale of the building that they don't have to honor the arrangements the previous owners had with us. We're so fucked right now, Brock." Brock asked him how that was going to fuck them over. "We don't have the capital to move. Not only that, we don't have enough money right now in ready cash to have a building put together the way we need it."

"Will they rent the building to us?" Harley just stared at him again. "Since I didn't talk to the people, I'm in the dark right now. Why don't you tell me who you spoke to, and I'll give them a call to figure this out since you want to be so snippy about things." He told his brother who he had spoken to and what they said about renting this building to them. "Why does that name...are you telling me that Katherine Archer bought this building so that she could evict us? That's about as petty as I've ever heard anyone be."

"You're pretty petty too, Brock. But the thing is, I have a feeling this has to do with Merce more than it does us. She's lied to them about things, and that is why they're not working with us. I've just thought of a plan." He told his brother his idea that only just then occurred to him. "We take Grandfather out of the nursing home and tell them that since we have no recourse without a rental or even a way to buy a place to work from, we're going to be putting him in a much cheaper run-down place. That should get her moving into getting us what we want. It's not like anyone likes Merce much anyway. She's just a child that sleeps around with anything that she can get to. I no more believe she has a college education than I have a million dollars in the bank right now."

"She does. Not only that, but she was valedictorian

of her class and graduated with a five-point grade average. I looked it up. Merce was only seventeen when she got her education, and then twenty-one when she was able to get a doctorate in engineering." Harley asked Brock if he knew how she'd gotten that. "Well, it's not like anyone is going to tell me she fucked her way to the top. All the college could tell me was that they wished all their students were as smart as she was."

Harley snorted. "I'm betting that's not the truth either. I do wonder at times how she's able to pull the wool over so many people's eyes. Next thing she'll have them believing is that she's the virgin she claims to be." Brock said he hadn't any idea how to check on that. "Me either. Not that it matters. She'd just sleep with some asshole and have him lie for her."

"When did we lose control over her? I mean, when she was just a baby, she would do whatever we told her, and there was never any fighting about it. Now that she's older, it seems like the more we try and do for her, the more she pushes back. Dad should have let us raise her when she was a baby. I think she'd be more like us and not this heathen that she seems to be right now." Harley told him he thought he was right and that she was out of control. "I think your plan to hold Grandfather over her head will work. I've never seen anyone so attached to an old man in my life. You'd think he was her guardian instead of us."

"We're not, you know. I know we told her that when she was younger, but it wouldn't fly now. She is supposed to be over eighteen now, I guess, so she'd be considered an adult anyway. However, that doesn't mean we can't keep trying to rein her in. Someone will have to before she gets herself knocked up, and we're going to be the ones that have to take her in. Lord knows that Father wouldn't be able to do it." Harley thought of something else. "I think we should consider having Father put into a home now too. There should be some sort of law that says that once you reach a certain age, you need to have an exam once a month to make sure you're in your right mind. I don't think Father could pass it now, much less in a few years. I'll look into that."

When his brother left him, Harley felt better. Not completely, but enough that he was able to make sound decisions regarding his sister and father. Calling the nursing home where Grandfather was, he was put on hold four times before anyone could talk to him. Explaining it all to the woman he'd spoken to when he committed his grandfather, he was satisfied that he'd be able to have his grandfather moved within the hour.

"Mr. Lowery, when we took your grandfather in,

you and your brother assured us that you had power of attorney over him. I have notes right here that say you were to have brought the paperwork in several times, but we've yet to see it." He told her it had slipped his mind. "So much so you don't remember that you don't have the power to make decisions for him? I've spoken to his attorney, and he said you put him in here under false claims. Do you know how much trouble we could be getting into over that if he was still here?"

"I'm sure it's a simple misunderstanding on— What did you say? If he was still there? Where is he if he's not in the nursing home?" She told him she wasn't at liberty to tell him. "What the hell is that supposed to mean? Where is he? You had better not have done anything nefarious to him. Or so help me, I'm going to—"

"Going to do what? You have no grounds to sue us for whatever we did for him. Nor did you have any rights to put that poor man in here without any kinds of extras. Do you know that he had to wash dishes for the extras he needed?" Harley said if they were extras, he should have to work for them. "You're a piece of work, aren't you? Well, I'm glad he's no longer here. The man needs to be treated better than you two ever did. If you want more information, I suggest you find him and ask. He's a lot smarter than you ever gave him credit for."

He was still talking to her when she hung up on him. Harley had a good mind to call her back, but his plan was out the window once he thought about what was going on. He did wonder who would have the nerve to take Grandfather out of a good place they'd put him in. It wasn't the best, not by a long shot, but it was a place to store him until he died. Harley almost hated to tell his brother. However, he knew he was going to have to. And he was going to have to talk to Merce too. She was behind all this. He knew it.

Pulling out his list of things he had to do today, he was surprised to find three envelopes with his and his brother's names on them. Since he didn't want to call him back into his office just yet, he opened the first one.

It was a letter of resignation from his personal secretary, June Baler. Not only was she leaving, but she was taking her four weeks' vacation as her notice. He wasn't sure she had any time coming to her — he never did the payroll but sent it out to be done. That way, he could blame someone else for mistakes. But to know that he had no one to answer his phone explained why he was having to do it today. Damn it, was nothing going to go right for him?

The other two were the same thing. Resignations

from his agents, also using their vacation time as their notice. There were sticky notes on them telling their schedule to show houses today and tomorrow. He supposed they thought he was going to do it for them. Well, he had a list of things to do, and it didn't include cleaning up their mess they'd made by quitting. Harley had a good mind not to pay them their vacation time. But he knew that doing that would cause him more trouble than it would be worth.

Before he was ready to take off to take care of his little sister, he had four more resignations and no one working. He was pissed off, more than he'd been in a long time, but there was little he could do about it now. First things first. Take care that Merce behaved, or he was going to have to take care of her the hard way.

~*~

Judy moved around the office slowly. Her body ached, and she was sure that had she called off one more time, she was going to lose her job. And wouldn't that just make Mark a happy person. Though she couldn't remember the last time he'd been happy about anything other than beating the shit out of her.

Every time the phone rang, she answered it with a smile on her face. Even that was painful, but she'd read somewhere that if you had a smile on your face, you'd be able to speak happily. There wasn't anything for her to be happy about, so she faked it like she did a lot of things lately.

"Hello, Judy. I'm glad you're back. How are you feeling?" Smiling at Del, she told him she was just fine and handed him his messages. Del looked through them as he spoke again. "Do I have anything going on tonight? After about five? I have a date."

"You do? Well, aren't you just about the luckiest man in the world. Who is it? The pretty little girl that's been hanging around here?" When his face turned pink, she laughed. It was painful but so worth seeing her boss embarrassed more. "So you and Miss Merce are an item, are you? I have to tell you, I think she's a perfect match for you. She's a right there in your face kind of person, and you're more of the lay back and see how things go before you react. Congratulations, sir. She's a good person."

"Thanks. She's coming in later to pick up some paperwork for a project we have together. Can you let me know when she gets here? I have about three billion things I have to fix up." He started away and turned back. "Are you all right? I don't mean to be rude or anything, but you look a little under the weather still. You don't have to be here if you don't feel like it, Judy. The place might fall apart a little, but you don't need to push yourself too much."

Tears, nearly always on the surface of her emotions, filled her eyes. Pretending to cough, she turned away from him to get a tissue. Telling him she was fine, really, Judy was thankful that the phone rang just then so she could take her mind off of how nice it would be to have someone like Del in her life.

Not that she felt anything romantic towards her boss, but he was a nice person, and she'd gone a long time without someone nice in her life. Putting her hand over her still flat belly, she wondered what she was going to do when Mark found out about this child. Would he push her down the stairs again? Would he beat her until she lost it? She was terrified that—

"Hey." She looked at Merce and saw the concern on her face. Staring at her for several seconds, Merce took her hand and dragged her to the bathroom down the hall from the office. Once they were both inside, she closed and locked the door. "Show me. Show me what whoever it was that beat you did to you, so I can go and give him ten times that much."

"I don't know what you're talking about." But she did. Merce just stood there, nothing written on her face but patience. "Merce, it's just fine. I promise."

"Sure it is. And I'm your uncle." She didn't move but stood in front of the door. "When I was seventeen, I had this friend in college that was being beaten by her boyfriend. Every little thing she did, he would beat her for it. If she got a good grade, she was fucking the professor. Had to stay after work, it was because she was getting a little on the side. Then one night, he killed her. Not because she was doing any of the things his mind told him she was, but because he was a fucking prick that liked beating the shit out of a person smaller or weaker than he was. Show me what he did to you, Judy. Then you and I are going to tell Del and David that you need someplace safe to live until he's in prison."

"I'm going to have a baby. If he finds out, he'll take it from me. He'll blame Del or any of the other men that I come in contact with." She asked if that was why she went with David all the time on calls. "Yes. For some reason, he thinks married men are above having affairs. Or maybe just affairs with someone like me."

"Someone like you? What the hell—? You know what? I don't care. Take off your blouse and let me have a look at his handiwork. After we talk to Del and David—because they're your best bet in getting someplace he can't find you—then we'll head to the hospital. All right?" Even though she was terrified out of her mind, Judy removed not just her blouse but her pants as well. "The mother fucker needs to be dead. Holy shit, Judy, how are you even walking upright?"

It was too much. Bursting into tears, she didn't care how much touching her hurt. It was wonderful when Merce wrapped her arms around her and held her. Merce didn't let go until she did. Then she helped her get redressed. It seemed as if she hurt more now that she had someone to confide in. Merce didn't even knock when she opened the door to Del's office and told him to get David in here right now.

It seemed like in no time, she was off to the hospital. The police were going to meet her there and fill out the paperwork to have Mark arrested. This had happened before, and she felt stupid about it. But Merce told her the only stupid person in her relationship was Mark, and he was going to pay big time.

"Are you going to kill him?" She had no idea why she asked the other woman that, but it frightened her a little that she didn't answer her. "Don't do it, Merce. You're the first real friend I've ever had, and I'd hate to have to visit you in prison. And Del would be so upset too."

"Yeah? Well, you're my first female friend too. Mostly women are intimidated by me. Go figure." They both laughed. The pain was getting out of control now, and Judy cried when the nurse told her she had something for that. "You rest, all right? I'll tell Del and David that you're in good hands. They're working on a safe place for you. I think you're going to be staying with his mom. That is a woman not to mess with. She's scary calm too."

As soon as the drugs hit her system, Judy closed her eyes. She felt safe right now, for the first time in ages. The baby, they told her, would be just fine with the meds they gave her since it was only a little bit to take the edge off. It was enough to put her over the edge, and she fell into a deep sleep.

When she woke up, she was in a different room, a pretty little room with pictures on the wall and a large television hanging across from her. Turning her head gently, she was happy to see Merce there, and she was with an elderly gentleman she thought might be her grandda. They were playing a game of chess.

"Who taught you how to play?" Merce told the man that he had. "You cheat. I didn't teach you to cheat. Especially an old man like me."

"You're only as old as you feel, Grandda, and I don't cheat. I've matured in my way of playing. You've over matured." She laughed when he snorted at her. "You know, I do that too. Snort when I think someone is full of shit. By the way, checkmate."

"Where?" When Merce showed him, her grandda laughed. "I have to let you win once in a while. Otherwise, you'd not want to play with me.

You should know that a friend of mine at the nursing home told me Harley called there looking to have me transferred. This friend of mine was sitting at the desk talking to the boss lady when the call came in. She sure did give him an earful. Wish I could have seen it. But then I'd be sitting in that place rotting away from the inside out."

"That's a disgusting thought you just put in my head. But I wish I could have seen it too. After they told me you had to work for the extras you needed, I wanted to hunt them both down and beat the shit out of them. Christ, Grandda, how did they come from the same two people that I did?"

"I don't know, but I'm surely glad as I am sitting here that you were born, honey. I surely am." Sitting up a little didn't hurt as much as Judy thought it would, but it did have both Merce and her grandda turning to her. "Well, hello there, pretty lady. We were thinking you were going to need a kiss from a nice prince to wake you up. I volunteered, but there were a whole bunch of men younger than me wanting to be the one to wake you."

Judy started crying, and the man left them in the room. Merce handed her a tissue, and she told her how sorry she was. Merce pulled the chair to the side of the bed and took her hand into hers.

"Grandda is all right. He sometimes forgets that women aren't used to being charmed. I have some things I have to tell you. Do you like it a little at a time, or do you want the bandage ripped right the fuck off?" She told her she didn't know. "I can understand that. How about we start off with some good news, and I'll sprinkle in some of the bad for you? That'll be something you can handle, right?"

"Yes. Is the baby all right?" Merce smiled and said it was. "That is the best news I've had in a very long time. Thank you."

"You're so very welcome. All right. Good news. Del is going to have you stay with his mom for a few weeks. The doctor said you'd need to rest and put your feet up. Also, someone will need to help you with the bandages. They stitched you up with about two hundred stitches. Some of them were to remove scar tissue that was causing you some trouble." Judy asked her if she had sprinkled her yet. "No, not yet. I'm working up to it for you. The police went to arrest Mark, and he was killed."

Judy didn't know what to say about that, so only laid there holding tightly to Merce's hand. She was speaking. Judy could hear her, but what she was saying was beyond her. Mark was dead. He'd not be able to hurt her again. Looking at Merce, she thanked her.

"I didn't do it. I wanted to. You have no idea how much I wanted to kill the fucker when they told me what you had endured. Oh, it's been about three days since you were brought in. You had surgery to remove some of the fragments of glass they found in your skull during x-rays." Judy told her how he'd thrown her through their back door. "Fucker needed to be dead a while ago. You all right now?"

"Yes. You don't understand sprinkling, do you?" They both laughed. "What happened to him? I'm sure you told me, but I zoned out there for a moment."

"He didn't want to be arrested, basically. Did you know he was doing some major drugs?" She said she had thought so but was afraid to ask. "Good idea. Mark was high when they got there, and he reached for one of the officer's sidearm. Once he did that, all bets were off. They didn't kill him then, but he did manage to try it again and got it. One officer was injured but is going to be all right. Another was killed."

"Whenever the neighbors would call the police on him for us making too much noise, he'd tell me after they left how much he hated cops. I guess before meeting me, his desire was to be one, but somehow I messed that up for him." Merce didn't comment, but she could see her mind working. "He wasn't always like he was. I mean, it wasn't until he found out I was pregnant the first time that he seemed to have changed. Like he became so jealous of everything I did."

"Men are like that. Women too, I guess. Men don't hold the patent on being abusive. However, now that he's gone, there are some things you need to be made aware of. Good things, I think." Nodding, Judy watched as Merce pulled out her phone. "I had to write it down so I'd not fuck it up. You had an insurance policy on you and your husband from your employment with Del and David. That will be cashed in as soon as the autopsy is finished. It's for five-hundred-thousand. Also, there was a rider on your house mortgage that says if either of you were to die, it would be paid off. The house is now yours free and clear." She looked at her. "Del's brother Peter has been working on things for you while you were resting. Your hospital bill is paid too. By Del. He said that since you had to work for him, you deserved a perk now and then. Let him do this. He and David both feel terrible that they never noticed you'd been hurt. All right?"

"Yes, all right." She told her again that she'd be staying with Katie for a few days. "I don't know her very well. Are you sure she doesn't mind?"

"I have a feeling that if she minded, she'd let you know." She put her phone away. "There is more, but

I think that's enough for now. Oh, you need to start taking some kind of vitamin for the kid. I don't know a lot about that sort of thing, but Darrel, another brother of Del's, has been in here a few times to see how you were doing. There is a warning stuck to the bottle that you need to take it with food. I guess it's very nasty if you don't."

"I think you saved my life." Merce said she'd only bullied her a little. "I know better. I would have kept going home to him and been beaten up. It's the only place I could go. There isn't a shelter around here. The ones in the other cities around here are full all the time."

"That's another topic I'd like to speak to you about. My grandda and dad need a project. They want you to help them get a shelter here so women and men can be safe when they need a place to hide out." She said she didn't know anything about helping them. "No, but you can help them in ways that only someone who has gone through this sort of thing can. Knowledge. Like on things they might need to put in. What sort of building do you think would help? They have it in their head that it would have to be a place no one would suspect of being a hidey-hole like a couple of condos that are close together. I think my dad has a couple of them. He's retired now and left me the business."

"That's wonderful, right?" She said it was, but she was a little nervous about it. "I believe I would be as well. I just thought of something—you were to have a date with Del. Did I mess that up for you?"

"You didn't mess up anything, my dear. We've been having food brought in here and getting to know one another over subs and pizza." Merce laughed. "I'm really falling for the man, Judy. Like, I need him in my life more than I need to breathe."

"I would imagine he feels the same about you. You two are perfect for each other." The two of them talked for a little while longer. The pain was starting to make itself known to her, and Merce noticed it. "I don't want to hurt my child, Merce. I've lost so many babies that I need to do everything in my power to make sure it makes it into this world."

"I'm going to give Darrel a call and see what he says." She did call him, and after putting him on speaker phone so Judy could hear him too, he told her that being in too much pain was far worse on the child than her taking a little bit of pain medication. "All right. I'll take it, but I really need to think about this baby."

"As do I, Judy. I want the best for the two of you. I understand what you've been through and how much this baby will mean to you. I swear to you, Judy,

I'm thinking of you both every time I put something on your chart." Nodding, emotional again, she thanked him. "No need for that. I'm glad I could help you out."

When she got the medication, it didn't take her under as it had before. Instead, it only took the pain down to a more manageable level for her. She was able to talk to Merce and even made plans about going shopping after she was able to get around. It felt good to have someone to talk to and not have to worry about how badly she was going to be hurt afterwards.

"You've never talked about Mark." Judy told her she wasn't sure what to say about him. "No, I can see that. He is still at the county morgue and will be released from there in a few days, I guess. We couldn't find where he had any family other than you in his life. Is that right?"

"His mother died some time ago. That's all I've ever—he has a sister. Her name is…let me think a moment. Heather. Heather Grey. I don't think I would have named her that, but then I don't know the family. She's not been a part of our lives since we were married, so I don't think I could even tell you where she lives. There might be some information in Mark's phone. I never had one, so I couldn't even tell you how it worked to find out." She said the police had it. "Oh. I guess they would. You don't think badly of me because

I'm not concerned about his death, are you?"

"No. Not at all. I've learned that people have different ways of dealing with grief. You might not even feel that at all right now. But it might hit you some other time. I want you to know, all you have to do is call me and I'll talk to you. Even in the middle of the night, Judy. I want to be there for you." Emotional again, she squeezed her hand. "One more thing I want you to know is that when you are ready to go home, you don't have to live in the house of horrors. The police went over the place and found blood, yours, all over it. We're of the opinion that you should just let it be sold. Me? I'd burn the fucker with him on a spit in the middle of it. But then that's me."

"Are you always this outspoken? If so, I think I could learn a few things from you." Again with the grinning, like she was very proud of her way of saying things. "I guess I'm sort of jealous of you being outspoken. I've never been able to do that. I might learn how now, but before, it wasn't safe."

"You're safe now." Merce stood up. "As much as I'd like to hang out here with you, I have a couple of things I have to do. It's tough being in charge, but I love it. You call if you need me. I'll bring food by later."

After she was gone, Judy watched the television, something she'd not done in a very long time. Not that she thought she'd missed all that much, but she did enjoy it. When her lunch was brought to her, she had to make herself calm down so she could eat. The joy of eating, a simple thing for most, was almost too much for her.

Judy was used to eating her meal from the floor or the wall after Mark had thrown it there. Sometimes she'd find herself contemplating eating from a trash can or stealing from a grocery store. Even if it was a single candy bar, it would go a long way in keeping her from being so hungry all the time.

Crying a little at that thought, Judy vowed that her child would never know the meaning of hunger. It would never know what it was like to be slapped around so terribly that you would wish for death. And she had, on more than on one occasion. Lying there feeling sorry for herself, Judy made a few more promises to her unborn child. One of them was that she would love it forever, no matter what it did or how it turned out. Touching her belly, something she felt free to do now, she whispered to her son or daughter all the things she wanted for them. The way they were going to live.

It was then that she made a decision about the house. It was a house of horrors for her. She might not tear it down or even burn it down with Mark in it. But perhaps someday, she'd sell it to someone that could make it a happy place. Yes, that's what she would do.

The next time she woke up, not understanding how she could be sleeping so much since she wasn't doing anything, Mr. Lowery, Merce's grandda, was sitting there with a pencil in one hand, the other holding what appeared to be a page out of a newspaper. He appeared to be talking to himself too.

"What is a three-letter word for spade? Well, if they're not going to even try making it hard, why am I trying to solve it? Dig." She told him what she thought it might be. "Hoe, huh? Well, that does fit with four across better. Thought I was going to have to shove some piece together like they do puzzles sometimes. How you feeling, honey?"

"Should I be trying to stay awake some?" He told her his missus would take a power nap, she called it, when she was expecting. "I guess this is a little longer than a power nap. What time is it, anyway?"

"Just after five." She told him she'd been powering up for four hours. "I would imagine your body is plum wore out some. It's taking advantage of you being laid up to catch up on some beauty sleep. Not that you need it. Nosirree bob. You're as pretty as sunshine in the morning."

"You really are a charmer, aren't you? You and

Merce must get along very well. The two of you are about as opposite as it gets." He told her that Merce was just like her grandma. "That's wonderful for you two then. I don't remember my parents all that much. I was just a little girl when I had to go and live with my grandma. She was nice, but not the mother I needed."

"If you don't mind me asking, what happened to your mom and dad?" She didn't know. Not a single reason came to her. "No one told you why you had to go live with your grannie? That doesn't seem all that right."

"They were forever in trouble for one thing or another. I just never thought of looking into it. I always thought that whatever they'd done, it was because they weren't the best of citizens. Much less parents. I'd be left for days on end when I was just a kid. But it was all right. I did learn a great deal about keeping myself out of trouble." She took his hand when he offered it to her. "Grandma let me read her books so long as I was careful with them. And when she passed away, she.... Goodness, Mr. Harlin, I have a house around here that she left me. I never thought about it until just his minute. I could live there with my baby."

"You sure could. And if it's around here close, I could be his granddaddy too. Well, great-granddaddy. I might enjoy that a lot, I tell you."

The two of them laughed and talked about what he was going to be teaching her unborn child. How he was going to be the best babysitter she'd ever found. When Merce showed up, she not only had enough food for the three of them, but Del showed up for food too.

"I don't know when I've ever had such a wonderful meal." They agreed with her, and she was surprised when there was a large cake to share as well. The rest of the Archer family showed up then, and she enjoyed that too. They were the best family to share a meal with, and know that you'd never have to worry about them having your back when you needed it. They'd be right there.

That night she was able to go to sleep without any drugs. Peter was going to look into getting her house opened up, and whatever had to be done to it. There was a trust with the house that would pay the taxes, as well as any upkeep it might need. It wasn't much, she remembered, but it would be all hers without the taint of Mark around it.

Chapter 4

Brock was glad he was able to go and have a little coming to Jesus meeting with his sister. There had been too much shit going on, and now she'd made it so Harley was in the hospital. He was stressed to the point he thought he was having a heart attack. The doctor told him the way his lifestyle was. It was a small surprise he'd not had one before now.

Not that he thought either of them were in bad shape, but he'd been told he not only needed to lose some weight—fifty plus pounds, he'd been told—but he needed to stop eating so much in the way of fast food. Like he had time to fix himself a meal at the end of his day.

Obviously, his very wealthy doctor had all kinds of resources that would cater to his every whim. Gyms, surgery. Brock and his brother were working men, and they didn't have time for cooking in the kitchen like other people.

He'd been trying for the last couple of days to get in touch with his father. The first couple of times, it had gone straight to voicemail. Not that he'd stoop to leaving a message. He was his son, after all, and figured his father would just simply answer. But then after that, it said that the number was no longer in service. What the hell was that supposed to mean?

Calling the cell phone company had gotten him nowhere quickly. All they could tell him was that the number he had wasn't working. Like he fucking didn't already know that. Nor would they give him a working number, not even when Brock told them their customer's son had suffered a major setback, and he needed to get in touch with him.

Going to his father's home first, he pounded on the door for several minutes before the lady that had lived next to them for years opened her door. He was wondering why she wasn't in a nursing home herself when she told him that no one lived there anymore.

"What do you mean, no one lives here anymore? This is my father's home, and I know for a fact that he'd be living here still." She told him he was wrong about that. His father had moved out several days ago. "That's ridiculous. Where has he gone if he no longer is living here?"

"You're the same little snot you used to be as a child. Even if I did know, I'd not tell you. If you were any kind of son to him, you'd know that now wouldn't you?" She started back into her home when he whistled to get her attention. "I'm not a damned dog, you moron. I'm going into the house to avoid saying something to you that the good Lord would frown upon. Now get yourself out of here, and if you were smart, which you've never been, you'd just leave those men alone and let them get on with their lives."

He stomped all the way to his car. Sitting in it with the air blowing over his face to cool his temper, all Brock could think about was how the world was going to hell, and he and his brother were going to be the only ones left with a nickel's worth of sense. He decided to head to his father's plant—if it was still in business. The thing had to be about defunct by now. All they did was pour driveways or some such thing. How many driveways could a city need? he wondered as he drove there.

Pissed off because he had had to park on the street because the lot was so full, he was rolling with a full head of steam when he realized two of the people that had worked for him were now sitting in a nice office with crap surrounding them. When his father finally passed on, he was going to make sure that shit was gone. Brock was stopped by a man he'd met before.

"Del Archer. You're not going in there. Your sister is in a meeting." Brock told him he wasn't looking for his sister but his dad. "Oh well, I think he and his dad are going to garage sales today. Something I guess your grandda enjoys."

"Why isn't he at work where he should be? Why he is still working is beyond me. He should be in a retirement home someplace out of the way." Del told him he was retired. "Not my grandfather, you moron, but my father. I asked you where he was, and I won't do that again."

"Well, that's good to know since I already told you. He's out looking at garage sales with your grandda." Brock rolled his eyes in such a way that there wasn't any way the man could not understand it was meant for him. "You really are a piece of shit, aren't you? But as I said to you twice now, your sister is in a meeting, and you're not going to interrupt her."

"What the hell is she doing 'in a meeting'?" He used his fingers to indicate to the man that he didn't believe she was in a meeting than he did this man was related to Katherine Archer. "I'm sure you might not know this about my sister, but she's nothing more than a slut."

Brock didn't have any idea how he ended up in

the emergency room, but there he was when he woke up. Not only was he there, but there was a police officer with him sitting there reading something on her phone. When he tried to sit up, his head felt like something exploded behind his eyes, and he quickly laid back down.

"Mr. Lowery?" Brock nodded but decided that was a terrible idea too. "I'm Officer Jacobson. I'm here to inform you that you are in the hospital and that there is a restraining order against you from Del Archer, as well as Merce Lowery. Do you understand what I've just—?"

"She can't do that. I'm her guardian. Where is she anyway?" The police officer told him he wasn't his sister's anything and that she was still pressing charges. "You. Did. Not. Answer. My. Question. Is everyone fucking deaf today? Why am I in the hospital? You can at least answer me that, can't you?"

"Sure. Del hit you in the face with his fist. Is there anything else I can do for you? I'm on overtime here waiting for you to—" He asked again where his sister was. "Now, how would I know? I'm an officer of the law. So far as I know, Miss Merce hasn't broken any laws. *She's* a nice person."

"And you're saying I'm not? Like I care what your opinion of me is. How can I get out of here? I have to talk to my dad and my sister. And I do too have her as my ward. My father has fucked up enough to make it, so my brother and I had to step in and take care that she was raised right. Fat lot of good that's done us. She's blown her chance for an education, as well as anything else she might have." The officer laughed. "I suppose you don't believe me? Not that I care, but I've seen her in action. She's just a kid, and she's stupid too."

"Well, that stupid sister of yours just landed a deal for the city to hire two hundred people to start with, then another hundred or so after the first training goes well. That kid, as you called her, is pretty important to our town right now, so you had better tread lightly where she's concerned. You just might find yourself in a heap of trouble." He asked her if she had just threatened him. "No. That would be ridiculous, don't you think, since I'm a law-abiding person. I'm just letting you know that people around here are thrilled with her work and will do just about anything to keep her happy. You remember that when you go around spouting off about how she's stupid from now on."

When she left him, he laid there thinking about the people of this town. They were going to ruin his chances of getting any houses sold if they kept this up. His name had meant something to everyone. He and Harley had worked very hard to not only make sure the town came to them when they needed to sell or buy a house, but they would also call them when they needed information about the town. He'd been lying through his teeth since they'd started out about how wonderful this town was, and now it seemed it was going to be a fact. Shaking his head as gently as he could, Brock reached for the little buzzer thing to get himself checked out of here.

He'd pushed the button for the tenth time when someone finally came into his little curtained-off area. The first thing the nurse did was take the call button away from him and disconnect it from the wall. Glaring at her had no effect on her disposition, as she was already spitting mad.

"You think you're the only one in here today? Do you have any idea how many people, much worse than you are right now, have been brought in in the last five minutes? You will need to wait your turn and —"

"I want out of here." She told him he had a concussion and needed to be watched for a few more hours. "I don't give a rat's ass. I want you to sign me out of here right now, or so help me, I'll have your pension."

She was still laughing as she moved out of the area, leaving the curtain wide open. Pissed off at the entire human race, he sat up and swung his feet over the side of the bed. Falling forward, he realized he was going to be staying longer and that there wasn't shit he could do about it.

The next time he woke up, he was tied to the bed at his wrists and ankles. He thought it was overkill on keeping him in the bed, but he didn't move so much as his eyes when the pain shot over his entire body like an electrical shockwave.

"You're pretty stupid yourself, don't you think?" The man stood up and looked down at him. "My name is Peter Archer. Yes, I'm related to Del. I'm here to explain to you anything you might not understand about your sister, father, and grandda. Not that I think you deserve to know shit about them, but that's not my call. What is it that has you willing to fall the fuck out of bed to find them? Didn't they tell you that you had a concussion?"

"Yes. Not that it's any of your business, but I need to find my father. He's moved out of his home and taken my grandfather out of the nursing home my brother and I have been paying for." Peter nodded. "Is there a screw loose in your head? Answer the fucking questions. That's what you're here for, isn't it?"

"If I'd not promised Merce I'd not harm you, I'd hit you again. Your father has moved out of the house because he wanted something that was all on one floor. Your grandda is living with him, and he thought it would be easier than putting him through going up and down stairs all the time. Taking the older man out of the nursing home has given him a fresh outlook on his life, and he's thriving more than he ever has. You've not paid anything on the nursing home for the last fourteen months. According to the home's records, you never visited the elderly Lowery, nor did you send him anything in the way of birthday cards or Christmas gifts in all the time he's been there." Brock asked about Merce. "She's now the sole owner of Lowery Construction. From my understanding, she's also going to change the name to Lowery and Archer. They're working together now, and it is a good fit. Also, you might not care about this, but my brother and your sister are dating. That will make us sort of related as in-laws if they decide to take it further. That won't keep any of us from using your head as a bowling ball if you get uppity again, but then you did ask about her."

"I forbid her to get married." Peter just cocked a brow at him. "She's just a child and a promiscuous one at that. I tried to tell your brother that, but he hit me instead. I should sue him."

"Yeah, good luck with that one. Are there any other questions that I can answer for you? By the way, you didn't ask, but I'll tell you anyway. Merce has moved into the house. Harlin turned it over to her just the other day." He'd have to add that to the list of shit he was going to take care of. "Also, you might be aware of this too, but my mom bought your building. Why would a real estate company not own their own building? Anyway, she bought it and is going to tear it down, so you don't have a place to work from. Most of your employees have come to work, in some form, with my family. I'm sure you know that. Also, if you think you're not going to pay them their vacation time since they told you they were leaving, I'll not just own your asses, but every little thing you've acquired since you turned eighteen. Understand me?"

"You're one of those vampire lawyers, aren't you? I should have guessed it. There is nothing you won't try to get a man when he's down." Peter laughed. "You think this is funny? That my being here in the hospital is anything that I deserve?"

"Oh yes. You deserve that and more. As for you being down? You've not yet seen down if you don't behave yourself and leave everyone alone. I'll make you have to look up at a worm if you fuck with me. Not only am I good at being a vampire of an attorney, but I will gladly take you down just so you can understand that I mean business."

After the man left, Brock realized he had no way of calling to the nurses to come and release him. Since he was still in a great deal of pain right now, he decided to let them slack on this for a little while longer. He had some thinking to do anyway.

His father had insanity in his family, so that would be all he needed to have him committed. And once he was in the nursing home, his grandfather would have to be put away as well. Brock was sure he could get his sister there as well. The way she did business was something that was frowned upon in most states.

He needed to talk to Harley. There were a lot of things they had to discuss. Like, how were they going to get on the good side of Katherine Archer? She had all the money, and that was the only way that he could see any of this getting fixed to their satisfaction. He still believed Merce was behind all this trouble he and his brother were having. Merce could be so incredibly childish at times that he wondered why he and Harley were the only ones that could see it. He'd take care of her getting married too. While he wasn't sure what he'd do about her in that sense of the word, he would think of something.

He thought about his mother and her way of dealing with things that upset her. Harley was starting to have those same traits. Acting the same way she had acted when he was stressed out. Rocking in his chair and talking to himself. Brock did as well, talked to himself, but that wasn't nearly the same thing. Working out problems by talking to himself wasn't the same as being insane.

Mother had been in and out of the hospital since he'd been old enough to remember. She'd be all right for a while, then she'd be this monster that would cry at the silliest things. Her temper would flare too, and she'd either beat him or Harley or lock them in a part of the house that was dark and scary. Most of the time, they'd be in the basement until his father came home or the staff would find them. Brock had always thought they didn't try hard to find them but said nothing more about it. His father had been upset with him for suggesting such a thing.

However, when she got pregnant with Merce, their mother was so different they actually enjoyed being around her. They loved going with her on outings, as well shopping at the big department store that used to make her have panic attacks much worse than the one his brother had had.

"Brock? Are you all right?" He wiped at his tears, not knowing he'd been crying. Seeing his father there embarrassed him. Knowing he'd seen something that no one other than Harley had ever seen had him snapping at his father. "You're not to talk to me that way. No matter how old you are or how big you think you are for your britches, you're still my son. Peter told me you wanted to talk to me. What is it you want?"

"This is all Merce's fault. She's the one that made Mother try and kill herself. When she wasn't around, Mom was fun. We did things with her that we couldn't before Merce came along. I hate her. I will always hate her." Father sat down in the room's only chair and told him he didn't mean that. "I do. I really hate her. So does Harley. Before she was born, we would go places with her. Mother was sweet and kind to us."

Dad stood up and jerked Brock's gown down, the snaps at the shoulders pinging around the room as they hit different pieces of equipment. As soon as he had it pulled nearly to his groin, he ordered him to look at himself.

"She did that to you, Brock. Your kind and sweet mother did that to you before your sister was even a part of her body." He looked at the scar that stretched from the bottom of his ribs to his hip bone. "Do you remember her trying to cut you open? How she had your brother lying on you to keep you down while she decided to remove the demon from you? Had the staff not hit her in the head with a pan, she would have killed you. You would have bled out when she removed your kidney, or whatever it was she was going for. She did that to you before Merce came to be your sister. Is that what this is all about? Your hatred toward Merce because you think she did something to your mother? How do you think that was even possible? She was four days old when she was put into the oven to be baked for our dinner by your so-called good mother. Christ, Brock. I just don't know what to say to you right now. If you want to talk to me, have someone call me. But as of right now, I'm finished with you and your brother if you don't get your heads out of your asses and stop blaming your sister for every little thing that pops into your fucking mind."

When his father left him, Brock thought of the day his mother had knocked him to the floor. She'd nailed his hand to the carpet with a nail gun she'd bought just for that very day. Then when he'd woke up, not only was father right about Harley sitting on his legs to hold him down, but Mother was stabbing into his belly over and over to remove the devil from him. Brock could still see the insanity on her face as she screamed at him to let it go.

A nightmarish replay of their mother played in his mind. It was as if his remembering the removal, what he'd called it, had made him remember everything.

His mother was insane long before Merce had been born. That was true. But she could at least come home sometimes to be with him before Merce had made them take her away.

~*~

It took most of the day to move the things out of the house that she didn't want. There wasn't much, not really, but Dad had wanted some of the things for his new place. Also, there was a bedroom of things that had been set aside for her brothers should they have a need for it.

"What is that stuff anyway?" She looked at one of the many chests in the room. After getting the thing open with Del's help, he looked inside of it and frowned. "It looks like every sheet of paper they ever drew on. Not to mention grade cards and things that might have been made in class. Why would you keep this?"

"Mom did it, I'm sure. My brothers would know, of course, but I'm not going to go and ask them. I was, however, thinking of the things I could do with these trunks. What if we had a garage sale and got rid of a lot of this stuff here and in the attic? Dad told me it's where Mom would go when she would hide from him. To be honest, I'm sort of afraid to go up there." Del told her he'd go with her. "Thanks. I might take you up on that. What time are our reservations for tonight?"

"Six. I didn't know a lot about what you like in the way of fancy eats, so I picked one that has a little of everything. I did notice you don't eat much in the way of red meat. You love a meat pizza. A contradiction, in the event you might not have noticed. You don't care for sweets all that much unless you're stressed. Also, you'll take diet cola over anything else being offered if you are given a choice." She grinned at him. "I've been paying attention to you for some time now."

"Did you notice I sometimes don't wear a bra?" He nodded as if he had broken his neck at some point. "I see. Did you also notice that when I know we're going to be alone together, as we are now, I wear a skirt? And look, no panties."

"You're playing a very sexual game here, Merce. Are you sure you want to go this far? I do, but this would be wholly your decision." She sat up on the nearest trunk and pulled her skirt up over her hips. "Holy fuck, woman, you're going to kill me."

"Good. Just being around you has made me wet nearly all the time. It's why I just simply stopped wearing panties. They would get—" His low growl was the only warning she got before he was taking her mouth, pulling at her clothing. Merce did the same to him. His pants were the first to go. She was glad he'd not worn a belt today. She had no idea how to take that from someone else's pants.

Her body burned once he removed all her clothing. When he stepped back, she thought for sure he was leaving her. It wasn't until he told her to lean back and said he wanted to see her entirely that she felt better.

"I've fallen in love with you, Merce." She stared at him and realized she loved him as well. "I've been falling a little more in love with you every day. Since you've been around, it's made me realize everything I've been missing in my life. I want you so badly right now I'm hard as stone, as you can see. But I want you to consider marrying me. I know it's soon that we've—"

"Yes. Yes, I'll marry you, Del. I love you as well. I think I was in love with you even before we met. I love you with all my heart and soul." He picked her up and took her down the hall. She was glad no one else was in the house—the staff had taken the day off to decide if they wanted to stay in her employment or not. Some of them had been ready to retire for some time, and she thought they were happy she was going to be living in the house now.

The bed touching her back made her realize he'd scoped out the house before she'd gotten here. The bedroom was hers when she stayed over. The bed had been made up, she'd bet, since the last time she was here, which had been a few days.

"I love you."

Before she could tell him how much she loved him again, Del was kissing her. Giving her more of his love with each swipe of his tongue, the touch of his fingers on her overheated body.

Her breasts ached and felt fuller. When Del put his mouth over her nipple, she could only cry out with it. Not in pain, not really, but with undeniable pleasure. As soon as he suckled at her breast, taking into his mouth, Merce came, screaming out his name. A wonderful heady feeling of love blanketed her.

"Again, love. Come again for me." She did so many times that she lost count. Her body, seemingly too exhausted to go on, would rear up and give him what he wanted. As he moved down her body, his hands making short work of exploring her, she felt her pussy soak the covers beneath her. "I'm going to stretch you for my cock."

Even the word sounded sexy to her. Cock. Something she had desired only from this man for what seemed her entire life. She held her breath when she felt him blowing over her heat. Del took his time making her wetter and wetter until he took her clit into his mouth and nibbled.

"Mother fuck, yes." She roared out her release. It came from her feet through her head and down through her throat. If she came like this again, she was going to die right here. Telling him that, he only laughed. Then he touched her with his finger.

It felt strange at first, like an invasion of her private parts. Then as he slid slowly in and out of her, she couldn't understand why she'd never had sex before. This was wonderful. Amazing. Awesome. There wasn't anything better than this, she thought. It was then that he took her clit into his mouth again and suckled hard.

She was on a boat capsized. Her body was no longer her own. Every part of her, every cell and drop of blood, screamed out for Del to stop but to go on. As soon as she came a third, then a fourth time, she knew she was going to die right there. There would be nothing to keep her from it.

As he moved up her body, she begged him to stop, telling him she couldn't take anything more. But he only had to sit back on his knees and fist his cock for her, and she knew whatever he did to her next was going to blow her mind. It would be epic enough that she'd beg him every day, every second of every day, for more.

"Don't tense up, love." She did what he asked,

spreading her legs for him when he moved over her. She was still tense, she could feel it, but he was gentle with her, telling her how much he loved her, how her cream tasted to him. When he moved his cock at her entrance again, she cried out when he pushed forward, breaking through the barrier that made her no longer a virgin but his other half for life.

Neither of them moved while she tried to deal with the pain. It wasn't as horrific as she'd thought it would be, but it was still painful. Moving her hips to try and get herself in a better position, she moaned when she realized he had moved with her.

"If you keep moving like that, I'm not going to be able to be a gentleman about this and let you get used to me." She looked up at him. His face was granite hard, the strain of him really being a gentleman taking a huge toll on him. Moving her hips again, watching his face, she rolled her hips upward and watched the stiffness of his face disappear in a kiss that he gave her.

It didn't take her long to come several times after that. Del seemed bent on making her enjoy this more than he was. When he pulled her hips up to meet his on his downward stroke, she held onto his shoulders as if she knew she was going to break apart. When she did, when she came with him, Merce knew that nothing would ever be the same between them. That they were forever and more a couple, no matter what others might say to them otherwise.

When she woke, she was alone in the big bed. She could hear Del talking in her bathroom and got up to see what he was doing. As soon as he saw her, he smiled hugely and pointed to the bathtub.

"I have to go, Peter. I'll call you later. I want you to tell Merce what you've been able to find out as well. All right?" She couldn't hear what Peter was saying, but it must have been bad. "I know you don't want to break her heart, but she needs to hear this. I know for a fact she loves you too."

"I do, tell him." Del told his brother what she'd said as she stepped into the warm water. As soon as she sat down, her body screamed out in tight muscles and bits of pain here and there, but nothing she thought she couldn't handle. Especially when Del sat on the commode next to her. "Do I want to know?"

"He found some things out about your brothers. No, you more than likely don't want to know, but I think it would go a long way in making what they've done to you easier to handle. How are you feeling? I'm sorry I was so rough on you. Your skin is very easily bruised, isn't it?"

She noticed them then, the small finger marks he'd made on her body. The marks of his teeth at her breast. Merce touched each of them, remembering what he'd done to her to have marked her in such a way.

"I'm going to think of them as badges of honor. Are you still going to marry me?" He smiled and got down on the floor next to her. "If you propose to me right here, Delmar Archer, I'm going to tell your mom that you seduced me into it."

"She'll just be happy that you're now going to be a part of the family." He pulled the ring out of the box and reached into the soapy water to take her hand. "I will love you more than I love myself if you'll be my wife forever."

The ring fit as if he'd had it made for her, but she knew he'd not. It was her grandmother's ring from when she'd been just a child. She'd seen it on her finger while she baked and made dinner for her when she'd go there. Grandda must have given it to him for him to propose.

"I love you, Del. Yes, I'll marry you and be your wife forever. But I want children. Not for the right reasons right away, but I want to see my grandda holding my child before he passes away. Your grandda as well. I want to see that more than I do the most wonderful museum in the world."

"Good. I'd like that as well."

They talked about the house. The rooms that would need to be updated. The stuff they still needed to get rid of. Every twenty minutes or so, he'd fill the tub with warmer water, careful of letting out the cold first.

They went to dinner after that, knowing that once their families found out they were engaged, they'd want to celebrate with them. She didn't care. Merce thought she was getting the best of all the worlds with their combined families.

Chapter 5

Peter hated the look on Merce's face as he showed her the pictures he'd unearthed. Bethany Lowery had had mental problems since she'd been a child. The pictures Merce was seeing now were from her file that he'd been able to get from the first home for the criminally insane that she'd been put in. Bethany had only been six years old.

"How did my dad not know this?" Peter told her it was because her records had been sealed. "I think someone should have told him he was marrying a murderer. Or at least told him to look into things about her parents. How was it known that she did this? Not that I don't believe you, but was there any doubt she did this heinous stuff to her own family?"

"No. She confessed, of a sort." She asked him

what that meant. "When the police got to the home, she was sitting in the front entrance playing in the blood of the dog she'd killed too. The police asked her if she was alone in the house, thinking like you do, that she was entirely too young to have committed the crimes. But she told them in a singsong voice that not only was she the only one in the house, but that she'd had fun killing the people that tried to boss her around. To this day, there are people out there that don't believe she did anything at all but was victimized by whoever had actually killed them."

Merce stood up, handing the photos to Del. He'd been hard pressed to do this today—they'd only been engaged since this afternoon. But Del had told Peter she needed to know it all, as it would help her make better decisions where her brothers were concerned.

"Was she able to stand trial?" Peter told Merce she'd been too young to see if she had the capacity to do anything like answering attorneys' questions. "I don't mean to sound cold, but I have a feeling from the other things I've been able to find out that she knew just what she was doing. Did you find the things I told you about Brock and Harley?"

"Yes. Those records were only opened for me because you and Del are getting married. They didn't want him to find out later that he might be marrying someone that could have the same condition. You couldn't."

She turned to Peter, waiting for an answer.

"Because, love, you're not my daughter. Hers either, for that matter." Harlin walked into the room and kissed Merce on the cheek. "I told Peter to look into that when he told me what he was doing for you. I didn't know it until much later after Bethany was gone, that she'd lost the child we created. But that didn't stop her from bringing one home. I think the hospital thought a child might steady her. It didn't."

"No, it certainly didn't." Merce asked him what he meant. Peter wished he'd not said anything then. "She tried to kill you after you and her were brought home. When the police arrived after receiving a call from one of the staff at the time, you were found in the oven with potatoes and carrots all around you, like you were a pot roast. Harley and Brock were tied to the chairs with their place settings in front of them."

"Christ." Peter felt sorry for Merce. This was coming out of nowhere for her. He couldn't imagine what his brother was thinking right now. When he spoke again, Peter was proud of him for not calling off the wedding. "What about the baby? Merce's parents? Didn't anyone say anything about a missing child?"

"They were dead." Merce asked her dad if

Bethany had killed them. "No. There had been a car accident that had taken both their lives. I promised I would care for you if they let me take you home. The doctors at the time thought if she didn't have a child to care for, all the good that had come from her pregnancy would have been worse. None of us thought she would go as far as she did. That's something else I need to tell you. Harley and Brock have blocked that out of their minds—the time before you were born. Brock was nearly murdered by his mother just months before we found out she was going to have you. When I told her she was going to have a baby, she lit up like she was back with us. I swear to you, had I known what she would end up doing, I would have left you at the hospital for someone sane to raise."

"Then I might not have met Del. No, you did the right thing, Dad. I swear to you, I will never think of you as anything but my dear dad." He hugged her then, and when Merce looked at Del, he was watching his brother. "I'm not who I thought I was. Does this make a difference to you?"

"Do you still love me?" She nodded and said with all her heart. "Then it makes no difference to me who birthed you so long as you love me. It does take your worry of having a mentally challenged child out of the picture. I know you were worried about that."

"I was. Very much so." Del asked her to come to him. "Yes, hold me. I'd love that, every day forever. Our children too. Dad, will you treat my children I have with Del any differently? Now that I know what I do?"

"Never. Never in a million years." Peter said he might. He'd never been an uncle before where he could be around the kids. "Well, son, I think you'll enjoy it as much as I'm looking forward to being a grandda."

Peter had been looking into some information about his cousins/stepsister and stepbrother. He didn't know why, but Mom seemed to be excited about it. That was all he needed to be all right with digging up the past with them. He'd not known how much they'd hurt their mother. As far as he was concerned, they could have gone to hell, and he'd have not lost one bit of sleep over it. But with Mom happy to find out about them, he would watch them so they'd not hurt her again. That was for damn sure. Peter was sure the rest of them felt the same way.

The rest of the evening, the four of them spoke of the things he'd been able to unearth. Merce took it very well, considering for her entire life, she thought she'd been the daughter of Bethany and Harlin. It was when Sherman joined them that things really started to fill in. He'd been helping Peter with all kinds of things, such as finding who her real parents were and seeing if there was anyone alive she could talk to should she want to.

"This is going to hit the papers badly when it comes out. Your grandparents on your mother's side have been looking for you since the accident. I haven't any idea why the police didn't come forward with the information they had, but since they didn't, I'm sure heads will roll from it." Merce asked Sherman why they'd been looking for her. "Your parents weren't married when you were born. Your mother was seventeen when she ran off with your father. His name was…let me look here. Your mother's name was Rachel Judson. Your father…here it is. His name was Chad Overlook. They were both killed when a semi full of logs from a logging company turned over onto their car when they were sitting at a light. There was nothing that could have been done to save them. Someone there delivered you from your mother's body before the ambulance arrived. There is some speculation that she was in labor when they were killed. The only way they could have found out about the baby was if someone told them. It wasn't in the newspaper. Not then, anyway."

"Where are they from? My parents, I mean." Sherman had that information, so he watched Harlin.

He was happy, it seemed to him, that this was coming out. However, he didn't think the older man knew about the parents and their wanting their grandchild. "So they lived out west in Vegas and were here to get away from their parents. Is there any way you can tell if they were justified in leaving home?"

"No. Your parents were just teenagers. Your grandparents were doting on Rachel, but they didn't allow her to run around. It seems she met your father at a party, and the two of them hit it off. From all accounts, they were in love." Sherman handed a sheet of paper to Merce, who handed it off to Del. "Your father had a good job while they were living out here. Your mother had finished school and then went on to college. She wasn't far from being an LPN when she was killed. Something that you should know. There is a huge reward from the logging company for your return. Of course, they paid out the ass for the accident too. Neither the money nor the insurance has ever been cashed out. It seems someone was waiting for you to find them and come home."

"I'm not sure that would be a good idea." Del asked Merce why. "I don't know. It's been at least twenty-four years since I was born. I can't imagine they'd be thrilled to find out that not only am I alive, but I've been right here in Ohio all this time."

"I have their contact information for you, Merce. And if it means anything to you, Mom was in the office when I was searching for information to give to you. She said she could be on her deathbed and want to know if a child of hers was still out there and doing well." Sherman looked at Peter, then back at Merce. "Chad's parents are still alive as well. Like your biological parents, they've been waiting on some kind of word that you're alive. I think if you speak to them, you shouldn't mention anything too personal right away. I'd leave that for when they decide if they want to be a part of your life or not. They, as you said, might not want anything to do with you after all this time."

"I would very much like to meet them. To tell them what a wonderful daughter you were to me." She hugged her dad after he sat down next to her. Harlin looked at Peter. "I know there are legal things that are going to be like a land mind for all this. What do we have to do if Merce should decide to contact them?"

"You don't tell them anything other than when she went to get her marriage license to get married, that was how you found out. The doctors that were there that night are all dead. Even the nurses who might have known about it are in nursing homes. The police for sure wouldn't have kept a record of it. So far as anyone knows, you came home with your wife and child, and that is all." Harlin asked him if it was legal. "More than likely not if I looked into it much deeper. I've not, in the event someone wants to know more than they do about what we tell them. Is it wrong? I don't think so. It's not hurting anyone for her to just show up as their grandchild. In fact, some might say it's best to leave sleeping dogs lie. Talking to them would entirely be up to you two. However, I'd never tell anyone, Harley or Brock especially. No one outside of this family needs to know shit about it."

"I agree with that one. They're causing enough trouble as it is." Harlin spoke to him about other things he'd been able to find out. Things that weren't good. Things that made his stomach turn a little when he thought about the other two's lives growing up with Bethany as their mother.

Merce still hadn't decided to call anyone by the time Peter was packing up his paperwork. Sherman hadn't given her the numbers he said he had, but Peter thought she'd do it if for no other reason than to give them peace. He knew it would bother her to leave the two couples not knowing about their children. Their only children, as it turned out.

Peter gave Sherman a ride home since he'd walked to Merce and Del's home tonight. Almost as soon as they were in the car, his brother started telling him how much fun he'd had researching the information on her parents. He asked him if he thought there could be a job in his firm for him.

"It's funny you should ask, Sherman. I've been thinking the same thing. How nice it would be to be able to find long lost people. This one is turning out to be all right. No one is dead yet that it would matter to. However, I have no doubt that someday it won't be so easy." Sherman said he'd gotten help from both Robert and William on this. "Did they like it as much as you seemed to?"

"I think Robert was just thrilled not being an attorney anymore. He was glad too when, like you said, it turned out well. I'm not sure about William. He helped a great deal with it, but he…. The other day I heard that he applied for a job at the local cinema. I'm not upset about it as much as I thought I'd be, them throwing away good careers. But I'm doing the same thing, so I can't say too much." Peter asked why they'd gone to college to be an attorney in the first place. "Mostly, it was because you did it. I think Mom being so proud of you for doing it didn't help. Not that I'm blaming her, I'm just saying that had a little to do with it. The other two? I don't know. I think perhaps, like us, it was a good way to make money and to make Mom proud of us. Grandda too. I was so jealous of Del when he seemed to go his own way. Even Darrel being a doctor didn't bother me like Del did. I felt a little like he'd betrayed us. Then I thought about how much he seemed to be enjoying his work. I hadn't felt like that since I was first in the office. I'm looking for that spark he has."

After dropping Sherman off at his home, Peter made his way to his own. They all, with the exception of Del, had lived away from home when Mom took that fall when she did. They'd all wanted to move home and care for her, but since Del had said he worked right in town and didn't have a home yet, it was perfect for him, as he had nothing to hold him back from staying with Mom. Every day, Peter wished he'd been able to go home too. Just to hang out with his baby brother and his mom without anyone else around.

He was getting that now, he realized. All the time he wanted to spend with all of them. Being an attorney was what he wanted, but the perk of being his own boss and being able to see his family without any trouble made it doubly wonderful.

Once he was home, he decided to hire himself a staff. His house needed a good once over and some updates. Yes, Peter thought. He needed to get his ass in gear and start inviting his family to visit him once in a while.

~*~

Brock read over the paperwork three times before realizing he didn't know how he'd gotten it. Looking around the room, he saw his grandfather there with Merce, as well as his dad and that man again. Del. Clearing his throat, they all turned to him, and he asked them what this was supposed to mean.

"I'm not your sister. Not even stepsister. There was a mix-up at the hospital, a horrific accident the night I was born, and the babies were switched. In a couple of days, I'm going to go and meet my biological grandparents on both sides of my family." Brock asked what the other paperwork was. "Oh, that's me suing you for treating me like you have for the last twenty-four years. Mostly it's from the time I turned eighteen, but there is a lot there that we've been able to find that you and Harley did. Like having someone spying on me all the time. Did you know that's against the law?"

"You're my sister, so I could easily get around those laws." Peter, he'd forgotten he was there, said it didn't matter what she was to them. It was against the law. Merce had been an adult at the time. "Like you would know. Did you get your degree from a gumball machine? Just sit there and shut up while I talk to my family."

"The only family in this room with you, Brock,

is Dad and Grandda. I've already spoken to Harley, who took it better than you are right now. All he did was toss me out of his room and tell me he knew it all along. There wasn't any way I had been related to you two, and he was finished with me. Which is just the way I wanted it. Nothing to do with either of you unless necessary." Merce sat down in the chair next to the bed. "You can make this all go away if you'd just sign the paperwork that says you'll leave me and my family alone. That you'll not bother me or the Archer family, and you'll not try and take Grandda away from us again."

"Ha. I knew it. You're lying. Do you think I'm stupid? That's you. He can't be your grandfather if you're not related to Father." She told him it was an honorary thing. "No, I won't allow that either. You're going to be my sister until I say differently. You've done all this to us. Made it so Harley has to slow down or die of a heart attack. I have to learn how to control my temper. I don't have a temper. The doctors are as stupid as you are."

Del laughed. "You're one short fuse from blowing the fuck up right now. What is it with you and calling everyone around you stupid? Do you like that word or something?" Ignoring him for the moment, Brock noticed that his sister was wearing a ring on her wedding finger. If he could have, he would have snatched it right off her hand, finger and all. He demanded to know what it meant. "We're getting married in two hours. In the event you were going to ask to go, I don't think they're going to allow you to be loose yet. Not with all the trouble you've caused around here in the last twenty-four hours."

"I don't know what you're talking about." He looked at the wall he'd been shoved up against when he'd tried to take out a nurse with an IV pole. Now he was on the psych floor, with a monitor on his ankle that he couldn't remove. Also, he had to be tied down when someone came into the room with him. "That woman startled me, that's all. I was going to see Harley when she told me I had to get back in my bed. I'm a grown assed man, and I decide when I'm going to go to bed or not."

"Apparently, someone with more intelligence than you thinks differently. Thankfully for the staff here." He thought his father's tone was a bit snide.

It hadn't yet sunk in that he was on a floor where his mother had spent a lot of time. He'd been to see her just the one time, and never again. He'd been afraid of her.

Father asked him another question he didn't want to answer. "What are you going to do when you get out of here, Brock? There is no more business for you to run. The money you had stashed away has gone to your employees for their vacations they had coming to them. The building has been demolished, and there is some nice grass planted there for future use."

"Father, you stay out of this. As soon as I am out of here, which will be sooner than you think, I'm going to have you committed like we did Grandfather. He will be in the room next to yours, wondering how it happened." Father laughed, telling him that wasn't going to happen. "We'll see. I still have a lot of pull in this one-stoplight town. When I'm free from here, we'll see who is going to be in charge of your wellbeing. You might want to think about that part. The worse you treat me, the same is going to be applied to you."

The nurse came to tell them their hour was up. Brock said he'd tell them when to leave, and she stepped out of the room and was replaced by the big burly man that had "helped" him take his shower this morning. The others walked out while he stood there and said nothing.

Father was the last to leave the room. "You could have had a good relationship with us, Brock. Especially Merce. I hate to say this, but you're just like your mother. Everything you do and say, it reminds me of her when she was first married to me." He thanked him. "It wasn't anything you should be striving for, son. She was locked up for the rest of her life, with nothing to show for it but two sons who think they're in charge of the family. You're not. You've never been. Merce is getting married in a little while. She'll have a wonderful family and be happier than I ever was. You should be happy for her."

"Why? She isn't anything to be proud of, Father. She's nothing but a whore and a slut. We should have let Mother kill her when she tried. Think how much better life would have been without her around. I know I'd be happier." Father just shook his head. "You know you believe me. I'm the oldest, and what I say goes. Just wait until I get out of here, and I'll show you."

"You do that. But also know that I'm not coming back here. I won't go anywhere you are for what you've just shared with me. To think that at one time I worried for you. Worried that you and Harley were going to be hurt by your own mother. Turns out, you're no different than she was. Just a little more vocal about your plans."

Father walked out the door and didn't say anything. Brock was fine with that. He knew he'd be back. He was his oldest son, after all.

~*~

They were packed into the office of the judge like

marshmallows in a bag. Del didn't want to pull at his tie again, but he was hot, nervous, and wanted to just be able to take a deep breath without knocking one of his brothers to the floor. When Judge Marcel came into the room, he paused at the doorway and laughed.

"How about we take this out of my chambers and into the main courtroom?" Del nearly knocked everyone over to get out of the stuffy room. As soon as he was able to take a deep breath, he felt immensely better. "You all right there, Del?"

"I am now. I was having a bit of claustrophobia in there." Laughing, Marcel told him they were big boys. "We are at that. I'm also a little nervous about this. Not that I think this is the wrong thing to do, but I don't want her to change her mind."

"She won't. My goodness, she's a pretty little thing. My wife came in today to see your mom again. They were fussing over Merce a little too much, and she sent them packing. I love that she doesn't seem to have a filter between what she thinks and says." Del said that was very true. "Well, now that we're all a bit more comfortable, how about we get the two of you hitched up? Before I forget to thank you again, I want to tell you how much I appreciate you taking Judy under your wing. She's always been a good girl, and I knew as soon as she married that ass she was going to be in trouble."

"I just wish I'd known sooner. I can understand why she kept it quiet, but if she'd come to us sooner, we would have made sure she didn't end up in the hospital so much." Del didn't mention the numerous miscarriages she'd had. It was hard on Judy, and he thought the fewer people who knew about them, the better she'd feel. "I'm ready anytime you are, sir."

It didn't take nearly as long as he thought it would to be married. Del had taken longer to figure out a suit to wear than it did for them to be pronounced man and wife. But Merce looked beautiful. He would never forget the first time he saw her in her wedding dress for as long as he lived.

It was a beautiful white lacy dress with no sleeves and short. The small veil she wore had been his mother's. Grandda had given him the wedding rings that had belonged to his love, and they had been set in all departments when his brothers gave Merce a bouquet of blue violets and baby's breath to hold. She kissed each of them before the service, then again after. Del couldn't have been happier than he was at this moment.

Tomorrow they were going out to see her grandparents. Peter had given them all the information he had found out about them, and they were about as prepared as they'd ever be. He was nervous about meeting them and what they'd say to her. But if they both turned them away, they'd have a good time seeing the sites and taking their honeymoon.

"Well, Mrs. Archer, are you ready to be my wife?" Merce told him it was a bit too late for her to back out now. "Good. I plan on spending the next few hundred years or so making you the happiest woman on the earth."

"Few hundred years? I don't know what sort of drugs you're taking to make that happen, but as long as I can spend them with you and your family, I'm game." He kissed her again as they waited for their table to be ready for their celebration. "I love you, Del Archer."

"And I love you, Merce Archer." Yes, Del thought, this was about as perfect as life could be.

Chapter 6

Ronny went to the door to answer it. Telling his butler, Cody, that he had it had the man standing nearby anyway. He didn't know why the man thought he couldn't answer his own door, but he'd been with them for so long, they were more friends than an employee to employer. Pulling the door open, Ronny stood there for several seconds, staring at the woman standing there until she smiled at him.

"Mr. Judson?" He nodded, not sure he could speak right at the moment. Instead, he didn't even turn to look at Cody as he told him to get Lily. "My name is Merce Lowery Archer. I've only just...do you think we could come in out of the rain?"

"Yes, of course. Come in." He nearly shut the door in the face of the man that had been with her.

"I'm sorry. I'm a little bit overwhelmed at the moment. Did you say your name was Merce?"

"Yes. This is my husband, Del Archer. We were just married two days ago. I didn't know about you until a few days before that." He nodded, feeling foolish until he heard his wife. She would have fainted to the floor had Cody not been right behind her. "I'm sorry for this. I guess I should have called. But I was afraid you'd not want to see me."

"You look like your mother. So much so, I thought for a second…. Come, let's go into the living room. I need a minute." Taking his wife from Cody, he carried her into the living room with them. Sitting in the chair with her on his lap, Ronny held her like the lifeline she'd been all their married life. "Can we talk until my wife comes around? She's not been well of late. Some kind of flu or something. At our age, it's dangerous to get a cold, and here we've had two this summer. I'm off my head right now. Tell me about yourself. Please? You said you only just found out about us. What did you do? How is it that you weren't at the hospital when we went to get our daughter? What—?"

"Ronny, give our granddaughter a moment to answer before you shotgun more questions than she can answer." He kissed Lily on the mouth, and she sat down on the couch. This child was his granddaughter.

There wasn't any doubt in his head about that now that his wife approved. "Tell me, child, where have you been all this time?"

"Ohio. Where my parents were killed. As I said, I've only just found out about you and the Overlooks. The night of the accident, there was some confusion with all the people involved, and I was mixed up with a child that was stillborn. My father didn't know either." He asked about her mother. "Sadly, she passed away some time ago."

"I'm sorry about that." She nodded. Ronny didn't know why, but he thought there was more to the story than she was telling them. But he didn't care. She was here, and he couldn't have been happier. "I can't believe you're here. I have been…. Oh, I must call the Overlooks. They've been looking for you as well. You've not been to see them, have you?"

"No. We came here first because you live in a house. They're in a gated community, and we didn't think they'd allow us in without some proof of who I was. I didn't want them to be hurt if they thought I was lying to them." Lily got up and came back with a framed picture of Rachel, taken a few weeks before she'd left home. "My goodness, I do look just like her. Look at her eyes. They seem like you could see right into her soul."

Ronny couldn't hold it back any longer and started crying. His granddaughter was home. She was here, and he was able to hold her, hug her whenever he wanted. Getting up before he made a bigger fool of himself, he was nearly to his office when the young man, he couldn't remember his name, touched him on the shoulder.

"I wanted to tell you something I think you should know. Merce hasn't had the best life growing up. Her mother ended up in a mental institution after trying to kill Merce when she was less than a week old. That was where she was when she passed away. Merce's brothers, older than her, have the same kind of condition. The doctors are treating them both, but it doesn't look good for one of them. Also, I love her with all my heart. My family does as well. I will never allow anyone to hurt her again." He put out his hand, and Ronny took it immediately. "I swear to you on my mother's heart that you will never have to worry about her being mistreated ever again."

"I believe you, son. I do. We've missed her entire life, you know. I know nothing about her." He grinned at him. "You really do love her, don't you? It's written all over your face how much you do."

"I do. More than I do myself." Nodding, he invited the younger man into his office as he made the call. While waiting for the phone to be answered, he asked the younger man how long they'd be here. "As long as you wish. We both work from home, so it's no problem for us to take a few days or a couple of weeks."

He wanted forever but didn't push it. Just then, the phone was answered.

"Did you know there are over three hundred kinds of hummingbirds in the world, Ronny? I was just looking it up to answer one of those damned crossword puzzles Holly does. How the hell are you?" He told him he was fine. Before he could get another word in about Merce, he started again. Chadwick rarely shut up long enough for people to have a conversation with him. "I tell you, Ronny, that woman gets loonier and loonier every summer. What did you need?"

"Our granddaughter just showed up here with her husband. Nice man. I can't remember his name right now, but he swears he loves her. Why don't you and—?" Chadwick asked him if he was drunk. "I'm not, and it's only nine in the morning, Chadwick. Why don't you and Holly come over and see them? She's the spitting image of Rachel."

"I don't know why I'd have to say this to you, Ronny, but this isn't funny." Ronny assured him he wasn't trying to be. "She's there? Really and for true?"

"Yes. She's right here in our living room,

Chadwick. Beautiful like my Rachel was, and as tall if not taller than Chad was. They wanted to come to see you but were afraid you'd turn them away." Chadwick sniffled, and Ronny spoke while his good friend regained control of himself. "She told me there was a mix-up that night. That a baby had been born to another couple, and it had died. In the confusion of the accident, there was a switch. They never told us there was a stillborn there. I don't know why, but after all this time, I'm betting no one would be able to tell us either. We have her here, and she'd really enjoy meeting you. Her husband too." Del told him his name. "Del Archer. That's his name. Come on over. But if you don't want to upset Holly right now, I can understand that as well."

"You know as well as I do that if I go there and it is my granddaughter, Holly will hang me out to dry." She would at that, but he didn't say anything. "I'll have to tell her first. You don't be surprised, Ronny, if we're still in our bathrobes when we show up. She'll want to get over there that fast."

"As a matter of fact, Chadwick, I'm still in mine. I'll change before you get here." He wasn't, but he thought it would make the other man feel better to think he was. "I'll have tea on when you arrive, the two of you. And some Danish. I think Cody can have some ready in no time. You two come here, but please be safe. She will be disappointed in you if you get yourself hurt before you see her."

"Is it really her, Ronny? I know I keep asking you this, but it would hurt my heart to think she might still be out there waiting for us to find her." Ronny asked Chadwick if he was near his computer. Asking for a picture of his wife, Del mailed it to the address Ronny gave him. "Damned thing. It takes forever when you're wanting something to— Oh Ronny, she does look like your little girl. Just look at those eyes. And that chin. That's—we'll be right there, Ronny. Right there."

They stared at one another as they sat there, Del and himself. When Del smiled at him, Ronny thought he could surely like this young man. But he had some questions of his own to ask, and he was a little afraid to ask them. He didn't know why, but he thought that whatever he asked him, Del was going to give him the truth as an answer.

"Ask me." Nodding, Ronny leaned back in his chair. "Merce will tell you right up straight if you want some information. I don't usually, but I have a feeling in this circumstance you need it more than you do half-truths."

"I do. But I don't want to know either." Del told him he could understand that. "Why don't you tell me some things about yourself, and that'll make me feel better."

"I'm the youngest of six brothers. My dad passed away not long after I was born. My grandda lives with my mom. The man who raised Merce, Harlin Lowery, is living in a condo now with his father. He's a good man with a wonderful heart. The two of them are getting along nicely. Merce and I are going to live in the house when we get back from here. It's being renovated with new paint and such. I have a doctorate in engineering, as does Merce. We're working on a project together to make mechanical arms for the operating room. It's going very well." He asked him about his mom. The smile on his face told Ronny a great deal. "She's amazing. Her name is Katherine Archer, and she makes the most wonderful jellies and jams. Her chicken and dumplings are the most tender you've ever tasted. She loves Merce as much as she does me."

"Katherine Archer the billionaire? She's your mother?" He nodded. "My goodness. I was just reading about her the other day. You and your brothers, you've been—you're Delmar Archer, the architect that designed the Watson Building in downtown Columbus, Ohio."

"My partner and I did, yes. I didn't realize it was this far-reaching. It was a fun thing to do for us." Ronny told him what he'd read. "That's what I heard. I don't know if I'd call it a modern miracle, but it does have a lot of *green* features that make it economical to use. In five years, the savings on electricity for the company using it will have paid for the building. And the city is paying them for the extra that they generate with the solar panels that were put on top of it, as well as in the parking lot."

He liked the way Del included his partner in the work. Also that he was modest about his design. There wasn't anything to indicate that he was playing him. As soon as he was able, Ronny was going to look into other things his granddaughter and this man had done.

They were headed back to the living room when the front doorbell rang again.

"That can't be Chadwick unless he ran every light on the way here." Opening the door, he had a feeling he was meeting not just Del's lovely mother but also the man who had raised his granddaughter. Pulling them into the house, he hugged the man first. "You saved her for us. I can't thank you enough."

"Well, I guess you realize it's your granddaughter." The woman, Katherine Archer, shook his hand. "I'm Del's mother. I wasn't going to do this, but I really had to make sure my children were all right. I do think of Merce as my daughter, and I don't want her hurt."

"Never would I ever harm a hair on her head

now that she's here." Katherine, Katie as she told him to call her, hugged her son. Then when Merce and his Lily joined them, there were hugs all around. "My goodness, this is wonderful. Chadwick and Holly will be here soon. They'll be so happy to meet you all too."

As they were settling down to breakfast, the Overlooks entered the room with them. Another round of hugs, as well as some tissues, were passed out. It was wonderful to have these large gatherings here. It made what could have been an awkward meeting much easier. Not only that but there was plenty of conversation to keep everyone involved. Ronny took Lily's hand into his as plates were cleared away.

"We'll need to sell this house and move out there with them. When the great-grandchildren come along, I don't want to miss a minute of their lives as we did this one's." Ronny kissed the back of her hand, telling her that he didn't either. "Oh, Ronny. It's like we have her back with us. The day we were told she'd been killed, it never entered my mind that there would have been a child too. It wasn't until later that they told us about her being taken away. I wonder, now that I know, how they didn't know to tell us the name of the person who had her."

"Medical science has come a long way, honey, but computer information even further. Had this happened in today's world, we'd know just where she was and how to get her back. But she was born in a time where things weren't as advanced as they are now." He watched Merce and Del together. "Also, she might not have met this young man, and that, I think, would have been a tragedy all in itself. They're perfectly suited."

"They are. So much so they do remind me of Chad and Rachel." She kissed his hand then. "Why did they leave us, Ronny? Do you think it was because she was carrying Merce? Do you think they thought we'd toss them out?" She asked him if they might have. "I don't know, to be honest with you. I mean, I'd like to say I wouldn't have done that, but I just don't know. We must have given them some indication that we would have."

He'd thought of that for years after finding out there was a child. Ronny wanted to believe he would have been compassionate and loving, knowing his daughter had made a simple mistake. But he also knew he'd been hard on her. Not that he'd ever raised a hand to her, but he had been hard on her when she'd stay out late with Chad.

Looking down the long table at the family there, he tried to imagine how it would be at the holidays with them all around a table. Del's brothers and mom.

There would be others, too, if he knew this family well enough. He'd bet anything that they welcomed all who were hungry to share the table with them. Every night too, not just at holiday times.

The longer he sat there thinking about his daughter and the young woman at the end of the table, who was currently giving Harlin a hard time, he wondered what sort of person she would have been had she grown up in this house, with himself and his wife. He had a feeling she had been better off with the people who raised her. Ronny could see himself making her crazy with his rules and being overly worried about her.

"She was better off where she was, don't you think?" He smiled at his wife and told her he'd been thinking the same things. "I thought as much. As much as I hate to admit it, Ronny, she is the person she is because she was with the other people. Otherwise, I think we would have smothered her. I think we would have done more harm than good."

"I love you, Holly dear." She said she loved him as well. "Well, I'll call my attorney tomorrow and see what we have to do about selling this place and moving to Ohio. I wonder if they'll have children right away or wait a while. I'm hoping for now, but I'll be patient."

"Sure you will. Just as much as I will try and be."

~*~

Merce read over the information she'd gotten from the private investigator she'd hired. It wasn't all bad news—there was just a smidge of good stuff in there—but she had a feeling Katie was going to be as pissed off as she was about this shit. Pulling up the pictures she'd found while digging, she didn't hear anyone come into the room until Katie cleared her throat.

"I can see by the look on your face that you've found some information you don't like. It's either information about the new contract you got or about the investigation you have going on about James and Mary." She asked her why she'd think that. "While I don't know your faces all that well yet, I can tell you're upset. Not just a little either."

"I am. You will be too when I tell you. How do you want it?" She said to just tell her. "All right. James's wife Patty died three months ago. It was a rare form of cancer they didn't know to look for until it was too late. She had a rough time of it, apparently, and it took its toll on a lot of people. Apparently not James, however. He's engaged." Katie asked her about the kids. "This is going to piss you off. Since the soon-to-be new Mrs. Pencil, Shelby, didn't want any children at all, he's put his up for adoption. He just took them to the department of welfare and turned them over to them. They've been there since a week after the funeral. I think he was fucking around before his wife passed away. Also, this will burn your ass. They've been living in Texas, not far from Mary and her son, for the last two years. She's divorced and currently trying to do the same with her son. Life, she told someone recently, is so much better without the trouble of a husband and child around. I'm thinking they both need to be shot in the head, but I know you won't let me do that. Not yet, at any rate."

"Are you making arrangements to go there to get them? Just so you know, I'm going too." Turning the computer toward her, she showed her the pictures of the kids' mug shots when they were taken into the department. "Oh, look at them. They look so lost. I think we should take a gun with us too. In case we need to put some holes in a few heads."

"Whose head are you putting holes in, Mom? If it's all the same to you, I'd rather you didn't. All right?" Del kissed her on the mouth and sat down by his mom. "Who are the kids? They're looking a little lost if you ask me."

"They're James's children. Merce and I are going to get them. Would you like to go?" He nodded but didn't ask. That's what she loved about this man—he was game for about anything. "The bastard couldn't even wait for his poor dead wife to be cold in her grave before he was getting married again. And since she's his new piece of ass, they've decided to get rid of the children. I'm going to take my gun so I can shoot his dick off. Mary's too. She's doing the same thing. Those poor children."

Del looked at her. "I'm assuming you have a plan that is less violent than my mom's. I hope so, at least." Merce told him she was going to be giving him a few minutes to explain himself. "Let me ask you this. Is there a reason you'd have to go see him? I mean, if he's taken care that they're not at home, it should be a simple thing for you to go there and adopt them. We'll raise them as our own."

"You'd do that? Of course, you would." Katie looked at him. "I did good in raising them, didn't I, dear? He's all ready to go there and pick up children he's never met and make them his own. I love that plan better."

"I'll go and talk to Peter. He can get things taken care of so there aren't any issues when we get there. I don't want to rain on your parade or anything, but this fucker sounds like he'd put in the adoption paperwork that you can't take them, Mom. Not that we won't fight that, but if Merce and I adopt them, there is very little he can do about it." Merce told him what else she'd found out. "So he wants them to go to any home without any thought to who he might be sending them to. I knew he was going to be a son of a bitch. This just proves it. I'll talk to Peter. You two, please come up with a better plan than the one you pitched to me. All right?"

When he was gone, Merce looked at Katie. "Would it bother you if we were to adopt them? They'd be your grandchildren again, and we'd do right by them." Katie said she knew that. "If we can, I promise you we'll bring the other little boy home with us as well."

"I'd really like that. To give them a good home. I can't help but think that things haven't been that easy for any of them. That little one there, she looks like she's lost her soul. I don't want any child to feel that way, but especially my sister's grandchildren. When can we leave?"

"As soon as we hear from Peter. I can make arrangements now for us to go out there, then we can be ready when we hear from him. However, I'd like for him to be with us when we see them. If only for the sole reason that he's an attorney and will have answers we might not have." Katie said she'd go home and pack up now. "All right. Also, Katie, I'd not take anything for them with you. I don't know anything about the home they're in, but I'd hate to take them something only to have to take it from them when we leave. We just don't want to cause any more undue stress on them."

"I like that idea. Very much. No, we'll go out there with the thought they might not come home with us and hope for the best." Merce asked if she thought she could do that. "No. But it did sound like I was doing really well at it, don't you think?"

When Katie left her to go home, Merce looked into flight times. Peter and Del arrived just as she was putting what she hoped was a good time to leave in her basket. He sat down across from her and smiled. It was, she thought, a good smile.

"I've been able to get a copy of the paperwork from the welfare board in Texas. There is a stipulation on the paperwork about the kids staying together, not being separated. Also, it doesn't have anything in it about any Archer taking them. I'd like to go with you if you'd not mind. To clear up any questions they might have." Nodding at Peter, she told him they'd been talking about that. "Good. I'll gather up the paperwork the courts are going to need. Having a marriage license as well as a good home will go a long way in getting them here. Also, have you thought about what impact this is going to have on the whole family?"

"Do you think they'll be mad at us for taking

them?" Peter just smiled. "You've told them, haven't you? You told them what we were doing?"

"No, Del did. But I think if you need support, we're the ones that are going to give it to you. Also, while I was talking to Ronny about his plans for moving out here to be by the two of you, he said we could use his company jet. I told him we'd take him up on that. That way, we can all hit the courtroom at the same time as a huge show of support." Katie said that was wonderful. All Merce could think about was how crowded they'd been in the judge's office when they got married. The men reenacted the way they had been packed in for her. "I'm going to make a few calls. In the meantime, it might be time to get their bedrooms ready. I wouldn't do much, not right away, except add in some bunkbeds to a couple of the rooms, so they at least have a place to sleep."

"My old room has that already. I'll go and see what we need in some of the others." After both men left her, she looked at Katie again. "Are you ready to help me be the mother of four children? At one time?"

"You'll do great, honey. If not, I'll shoot you and take them for myself."

Merce was still sitting there when Del touched her shoulder. After telling him what his mother said, all he did was laugh. She didn't think she'd been kidding.

Getting the rooms sorted out was much easier than she'd thought it would have been. Sobie, their new cook, said she had a son about the age of her new children. Carter, just shy of his seventh birthday, came over and told her what he thought she should put into the room. A computer was high on his list, as well as giving them the space of different rooms later. If he was right, she was going to buy him a computer too. Merce might even do it if he turned out to be wrong. But when he turned to her and looked serious, she knew the kid was going to go places when he grew up.

"Don't push them, Mrs. Archer. I have a friend in school that was adopted when he was five. Everyone always asks him what it was like to live with people he didn't know. I thought he didn't like that, so I didn't ask him. We're best buds now because he'd come to me when he'd had enough. His new mom? She's too clingy, he told me. And the dad is trying to make him a sports lover." His face told her that Tom didn't care for sports much. "They'll need space, and to be able to know they can come to you. You don't have to keep asking them if they need you. They'll figure you out."

"Have you figured me out, Carter?" He looked at her from head to toe. She didn't think he was just making himself look reflective either. "I've never had a child before, much less four of them."

"You're a nice lady, and you're smart. You can help with their homework without making them feel stupid. You didn't me when I came in here and told you to get rid of the girly rugs." She told him she'd have not noticed them. "No, and that's another thing I want to tell you. Kids are way smarter than you think we are. We know things that would make your hair turn white, as my grannie says all the time."

She wondered what Carter knew but didn't ask. Giving him space, she hoped he'd come and hang around with the kids too. Merce gave him ten dollars for his help and told him he could have whatever he wanted for his room. Or his sister's, if he wanted it.

"Thanks. I know you're going to use the bunk beds for the girls, but if you get rid of them, I'd like them. When I have a sleepover, there ain't nowhere for everyone to sleep."

Merce was going to get him a set. In the few minutes he was there, Carter had taken a great deal of worry off her. She could do this. A least she hoped so. If not, then she'd ask for help. There certainly was plenty of it to go around, she thought with a laugh.

Chapter 7

Merce didn't want to make this call, but she'd made a promise, one that she intended to keep. As she pushed in the numbers, she thought of how she was going to tell this woman that her brother was gone, and though he'd already been cremated, his ashes were not going to be picked up by his wife.

"Hello." The voice sounded happy, almost too cheerful, and Merce hated this even more. Asking to speak to Heather Grey, she heard the other woman laugh. "This is her. You can tell me anything you want, but I'm not buying anything. That gets me into trouble."

An odd way to answer the phone, she thought, but Merce began speaking. "I'm sorry, Ms. Grey, but I'm calling to let you know that your brother is dead.

He was killed several days ago."

Not knowing what to expect, Merce jerked the phone from her ear when Heather began wailing and screaming about her brother. The pain in her voice was palpable. She either hadn't heard Merce telling her she was so sorry, but she had more information or was ignoring her. It wasn't until another voice sounded that Merce listened to the newcomer with more interest.

"What the fuck, Hey-hey? What's the matter with you?" In a babbling voice, Heather explained to the other woman that her brother was dead. "Yes, he is. It was my dad. Why are you—? Is someone on the phone talking to you?"

"Yes. She said he was killed." The other voice said he'd died a while back, and there wasn't any reason for her to bet getting upset now. "Oh. I guess I don't need to be crying either, huh?"

"No. It's been a long time. Who is that you're talking to?" Heather told her she didn't know who was on the phone. "Why don't you let me have it, and I'll figure it out for you? That way, you can go and eat your breakfast and get ready for your job."

"Okay." The singsong voice told Merce she might well have had the wrong person. "I'm going to have to tell Mr. Watson I got to answer the phone. Maybe he'll let me answer it at work."

"Don't count on it, Hey-hey. You did get upset for nothing. Go eat, and I'll take you to work." The voice of the stranger was soft. Playful to Heather. But when she spoke to her, Merce could tell how protective she was of the other woman. "What the fuck are you calling here for and upsetting Hey-hey? Whoever you are, you'd better believe she isn't going to be harmed by your shit again. Do you understand me?"

"She's mentally challenged, isn't she?" Merce didn't know why she'd said that aloud, but she knew it to be true. "You're the Heather Grey I think I was supposed to talk to. I thought the other woman said she was Heather, but I don't know for sure now. Are you the sister of Mark Grey?"

"She is Heather Grey as well. I'm her niece. And yes, I'm the sister of Mark Grey." Before she could tell her the news, Heather began speaking again. "Mark is dead then. I guess I assumed it was a scam to get my aunt to give you money. Not that it matters to you, but you're right on her being challenged. Thank you for that, at least—not calling her retarded. What happened to Mark?"

"He was being arrested for several things at once but grabbed an officer's weapon two different times. The second time he killed an officer at the scene. The second officer died later of his wounds. Mark was killed justifiably." She said she didn't doubt it. "You're aware, I'm assuming, that he was married."

"Yes. Judy Grey. I've never met her. Mark would call here, telling me about the shit she was supposed to have done to him. I didn't believe it, of course. Mark could never tell the truth because a lie was easier for him. Is she dead?" Merce told her she was in the hospital but doing much better. "He told me he had to knock her around a little. I would have helped her, but I had had enough of his shit when he was living around here. And my aunt had as well. Besides, my thinking was if she didn't want to be knocked around, she should have gotten herself a gun and blown his fucking head off. But then, that's just me. What else did you want? If you think I'm going there for any reason, then you can get that shit out of your head right now. I don't now or ever want to have anything to do with Mark, or his death, for the rest of my life."

"What about your sister-in-law? She might need you." Heather told her that she had enough dealing with her aunt. "You're caring for her then?"

"I am. I have been since I was eighteen, and she needed someone other than a nursing home, which would take what little money there was for her. Or I should say what little money was allotted to her. My father thought she was a burden, just not his." Merce told her she was sorry. "No worries on your part. Hey-hey and I are getting along just fine on our own. So you can understand why we're not going to be sucked into any drama. We have enough here on our own."

"I guess I can understand that. Judy is the one that asked me to find you and let you know that Mark was dead. Also, she's going to have a baby. There had been many before this one, but without Mark around to knock her about, she might be able to bring this one to term." There was silence on the other end, but Merce thought she might not get a second chance to tell the other woman this. "There was insurance as well. I'm not entirely sure how much there is, but Judy should be all right."

There was very little noise in the background. Merce might have thought she'd been hung up on but for the singing from Hey-hey, that she could hear. Just as she was going to ask Heather what was going on, she spoke again.

"Hey-hey and I will be there in a few days. If you can stop her from getting the insurance, I'd appreciate it. I don't want any of it. I'm going just fine on my own here, but if Judy is saying she's having my brother's child, she's lying." The line was cut off this time, and it left Merce with more questions than it did answers about a great many things. Putting her phone on the desk, she sat there staring off into space, letting her mind think about what was going on with Judy and Mark.

"Are you all right?" She kissed Del when he interrupted her thoughts. Smiling at him, she thought of the best way to ask him what was forefront in her mind. "What is it? You know you can ask me for the moon, and I'll give it to you."

"That's just what I need. The moon in my pocket." Kissing him again, she stood up and asked him to have a seat. When he was settled, she sat on his lap. "Now, I want you to think about this before you say anything. Do you trust Judy Grey? I mean, in all the time she's worked for you—how long has that been?"

"Just over five years, I guess. And do I trust her? I've had no reason not to have trusted her. Why are you asking?" She told him of the conversation she'd had with Heather. "So she didn't explain what she meant by that. Do you think there is a cause for her to be suspicious of Judy? As I said, I've not had a reason to not trust her. However, we never let her into our accounts. There was never a time when she was in charge of the money, nor did she go to the bank for us. At least that was what we said. I'll talk to David and see what he has to say."

"Could you do it now? I don't know why I think

Heather is telling me the truth, but I do. There hasn't been any reason for me to not trust Judy like you said, but now that it's been put out there, I'm a little wary of what Heather might mean." He picked up the house phone he used instead of his cell. She'd noticed he did that when at home. Del would put his phone near the front door rather than carry it around. "Don't tell him what I'm thinking. Just sort of work up to it."

"Hey, David. Merce was just talking to Judy's sister-in-law and wonders if there is any reason for us not to trust Judy." She smacked him on the chest, and he laughed. "She told me to work up to it, but I thought this way was better. We don't beat around the bush anyway. I think we've been friends too long for that." He paused again. "Yes, I can put it on speakerphone. Merce is right here with me."

"Merce?" She said she was there. "It's funny you should be asking about that today. I just got my bank statement from my personal account, and there is just over ten grand missing. I've called the bank, and they're looking into it. I don't normally keep that much in there, but my wife and I are thinking of getting a boat to do some traveling with, and it's not there. I've checked with my wife, and she said she would never do that. She wants to go boating as much as I do."

"Did you ever give Judy your account

information?" He said he'd not. "Do you leave out your checkbook? Something she could use to get the information she'd need?"

"No." Then she heard his fingers snap. "Wait. I didn't use her for banking, but there was one time when there was an issue about my mail she got from the post office for me. When we were first using Judy to go to the post office to get company mail, she picked up mine as well. When I got it from her, there were several envelopes open. Two were credit card offers, and one of them was my statement. I never thought of it again until just now. Do you suppose she did it then? Got what she needed to use?"

"It would certainly make it so you'd not be suspicious of her if it turned up now." Asking him to hold on, she called Peter to have him come over and see what he could make of it. "Peter said for you to put a seal on your account. He also wants to know if the money was taken out all at once or over a period of time."

"All at once." She relayed the information to Peter. "This is insane, Del. I mean, she's been working for us for about five years now, right? Why now? And I'm assuming you found the same thing."

"I've not, no. But as I said, Merce contacted Mark's sister, and she wasn't coming here until she heard there was insurance. I'm not sure why it was the mentioning of the baby, but that got her coming here, and I think that's a good thing." David answered a few more questions for her as he spoke to Del. "Was there any time when we sent her to the bank for the company that you remember? I don't. Not even to give her a credit card to order supplies for the office when she needed them."

"We didn't even open an account she could have used." Things started to fall into place while speaking to Peter and listening to the men. This woman was far smarter than anyone thought. Peter even said that Del and her should put a hold on their accounts too. At least until they found out more about Judy. "I'm going to look into some things here in the meantime. Until you hear from me or Merce, I'd not let her even go to the post office for the company anymore. It's much too dangerous feeling now."

David agreed, and when he hung up, Del looked at her. His face told her a great deal. He didn't care for not trusting someone that worked for him. Also, she'd bet anything that his mind was working on other things he'd seen but not noticed until he had to think about them.

"Peter is going to have someone look into her life. Also, other things, like if her name really is Judy. I'm worried more about David than I am us." Del told her that David was going to be all right too, or he would have told him differently. "I'm glad to hear that. No one wants to feel they've been cheated. Especially if she's been playing him for the last few years."

"Did you ask her what she meant by what she said?" Merce told him she'd never gotten the chance. "I see. Well, I don't, but I can understand how you came to see what we know. I can make a call or two. If I were to call my mom, she'd be able to find out a great deal. She's been in this town all her life, and she might just be able to make a few calls of her own and find out exactly what Heather is talking about."

"What if it's nothing more than a sister-in-law that is out to make trouble?" He asked her if she thought that was the case. "No. As I said, I don't think Heather was going to come here at all until I mentioned the baby. For all we know, there might not even be one of those. Or worse yet, there never was a child at all. She didn't tell us how many she'd lost, but I would think it would be something a woman would just know. Not just how many, but the date and time as well. I would, I think. By the way, we need to get ready to go and see to the kids tomorrow. I don't want them to have to stay in that place any longer than they have to."

The plan had been to go and get the kids a few

days ago, but they had to wait on paperwork to be completed. Mostly it was to prove they were related to the children and could afford to take all four of them into their home. Even Peter wanted things to go well for them, and he'd been working nearly nonstop in getting everything ready. Tomorrow they had an appointment to meet the kids, then later in the day to meet with the judge.

"I'm not wearing a suit, as you suggested. Neither is Peter if he gets to see the kids as well." She nodded, telling him they might be frightened by the sight of such huge men in suits. "I don't know why, but I think you're just telling me that to make me feel better."

"No. I've looked at the paperwork on your cousin. He's only five feet six inches tall, and a hard wind would blow him away. You guys aren't nearly that tiny, and it might be too much for them." Del told her he thought she was correct. "You had better be learning to say that more often. I'm nearly never wrong."

They were both laughing as they headed to dinner. Tonight it was just the two of them. Merce was about as excited as she'd been in some time to have dinner alone with a man. Especially this one. He was, as far as she was concerned, the best man in the world.

~*~

Todd held his two sisters' hands as they waited in their room. Brian was with them, but he wasn't allowed to get up and move around too much. He'd come to the place with a broken leg a few days ago, and it was still painful for him. Brian told him that his mom's new husband had beaten him up when he wanted to go out to dinner with them. He told him they left him at home all the time with just cold pizza and soda pop. Soda pop was something that none of the kids liked.

"Who do you think they are, Todd?" He told Amy he didn't know, but they were going to have to be quiet, or they'd be put to bed again without supper. "I know. But these people, do you think they're going to ask us questions that will make us cry? Poor Jane didn't like being told she wasn't going to get to go back home ever again."

He didn't either. But that was what the police had told them two days after they arrived here. That their father had turned their care over to the orphanage, even though they weren't orphans, and said he didn't want them anymore. Every time he thought of that, it made his heart hurt more. His momma had died, then his daddy said he didn't want them.

Not that he didn't believe he'd say that about

them. Since their momma had died, their father had been saying all kinds of things to them. Like he didn't want them. That they were the scourge of the earth. He'd had to look that word up, and it dug into his heart that someone would say that about their own kids. Todd could still see each word as he had read it to his sisters.

A scourge is like being the scum of the earth. There was nothing worse than being called a scourge. Low as a thing could get. A disgrace to the world. Nothing or anything. Just flat-out gross.

When the door opened to their room, he and his sisters stood up.

"You'll behave yourself, or you'll not have dinner again, do you hear me?" They nodded. "And you'll not be whining and blustering about how you want to go home. I told you, and that officer told you. He doesn't want you anymore. None of you. Your father has moved on, and you should as well."

"Yes, ma'am." Todd watched as they wheeled Brian into the large room. He thought it was funny that this room was the only one that was decorated. The rest of the rooms looked as bare as the trees did in the winter. But he also knew that when spring rolled around, the rooms would be the same, and the trees would be pretty again.

They were seated just as two women and two men came into the room with them. The younger woman smiled at them, but he was afraid it was a trap. Everything was a trap nowadays. Every move he and the others made was thought of over and over to look for traps and such to get them into some kind of trouble. He was sick to death of not having food when he wanted it. Or being able to talk about anything that he wished with his sisters. Even Brian, who he'd only heard of until the other day, was someone he wanted to talk to.

"My name is Merce Archer." Todd squeezed tightly on his sister's hands. When she squeaked, he let them go and stared at the woman when she laughed. "I take it you know who the Archers are. I'm sure you've heard all kinds of terrible stories about the person. Is it Katie? Katherine Archer that you're afraid of?"

Todd wanted to tell her but looked around the room. The people, all four of them, looked as well. Then the big man sitting next to Merce stood up. Todd felt his butt tighten up so tight he was afraid it would never open again.

"We'd like to speak to the children alone." The woman that had brought them into the room said that wasn't allowed. "I'm sure under normal circumstances you don't allow it, but that's what we're going to do.

Or you can allow us to take them out to dinner, as we said we were going to do when we got here, without any trouble. That is still going to happen, by the way. As soon as the police arrive."

"Why is it that every time someone comes here, they think to change the rules to suit themselves? I've explained to you that we don't allow the children to have time alone with people we don't know. Also, leaving this facility is against the rules for all children. You'll just have to deal with me being in here and not taking them anywhere. As I have told you twice now."

When the police arrived, the children were led out to a long limo and put in the back with the big people. Even Jane had a nice car seat, and Brian was put into a special harness thing that held him still while they were getting ready to leave. It all happened so fast that Todd wanted to stick his tongue out at Mrs. Shelby and give her the finger. Not that he'd ever done that before, but he thought this was a good time to start. Instead, he and the others just sat there holding hands.

"Now. I want you to know that this is your great Aunt Katie. Her sister was your grandma. Not that you ever met her, but that's who she is. She also raised James and Mary when they were smaller, and their mother and father died." Todd knew that but kept his mouth shut. "You can talk freely if you want. No one here will say a word to that old bat."

"She's mean." Todd tried to shush his sister Amy. "She is. You know it too. We might not get any dinner for the next hundred years, but that don't change up that she's mean to us."

"You must be Amy." Amy nodded at Merce. "I'm happy to hear that you guys haven't had your tongues cut out. As I said, you can say what you want. Also, I want you to be aware that there will be no more skipped meals for you. I'll take care of her if she tries that."

"I believe you." The adults laughed at Brian, but none of them thought it was funny. They were trapped as surely as if someone had stuck them into a cage and never was going to let them go home. "My mom said I wasn't going to do her any good with me hanging on her tit. I had to ask Todd what it meant. She's not all that nice either. Uncle James told her what he was doing with his kids, and she thought she'd do the same. My daddy said she was a follower but wasn't smart enough to think up anything on her own."

"That's about right. However, can you tell me why your father didn't come and get you, Brian?" He told her about the divorce and what the lawyer told her. "Did your dad ever try and harm you?"

"Nah. He and me, we were buddies. But he's

away now. I think he's in a place called Gurwanda. I don't know where that is, but I heard my mom telling Uncle James that she'd taken care that he was never coming home. None of us are going to get to go back to our homes." Merce asked Brian if it was called Grenada. "Yeah, that's it. He is stuck there without papers. I guess I can understand that. My mom had all the stuff in his office burned up the day he left on a business trip. Then she told me he had left us. I didn't believe her. Dad would never leave me without saying goodbye and giving me a hug."

While Brian cried, Todd watched the two men. When one of them put out their hand, he flinched from it, sure he was going to be hit again. The man seemed angry for a second or two, then he smiled. It was tight like he was still mad, but he didn't yell at him.

"I'm not going to hurt you. I'm assuming you've been hurt by someone recently." Todd looked at his sisters, then back at the man. "You don't have to worry about any of us harming you guys. And I can swear to you that I'll kill anyone that tries."

"I've heard that before." He nodded to his cousin. "His mom's boyfriend thought it would be fun to break his leg before they brought him to the orphanage. My father would knock us around enough he'd have to take us to the hospital. We were never allowed to say anything like it happened, so we learned really early not to trust anyone."

"Do you know that I came to see you once?" He barely remembered the older lady, but for some reason, he'd been told not to ever trust an Archer. "I see by your face that you were told about me and what a horrible person I was to your father. He isn't a nice man. But these two men are my sons. And this is my son Del's wife, Merce. My name is Katie. You can call me aunt if you wish, but I'm hoping that after today you'll be my first grandchildren."

He didn't understand how that worked. Since he'd never met any of his relatives before, he wasn't sure of a lot of things. However, Todd didn't think that just because you were an aunt to someone, you eventually became a grandma.

"We'd like to take you home with us." Todd sat there for a minute or two before realizing they were waiting on him to get out of the limo. Sure they were going to be back at the home. He was tense until he realized they were in front of a restaurant, one he'd never been to before. Del got down on one knee and looked at all four of them. "I've just been thinking that this isn't going to be a place you're going to enjoy. I was thinking steaks, but I'm now wondering if you'd like a pizza or some burgers more."

"Burgers. I love hamburger without any cheese on it, but cheese on my French fries." He looked at Amy when she spoke. "Well, I do. What do you want to eat? Whatever they plop down in front of you like they do at that place? If they take our food from us for being here, don't you want something you'd like to remember?"

"I don't want you or Jane to be without at all." She hugged him, and Todd felt his eyes fill with tears. "I love you guys, and I don't want you to starve because of this night, Amy. You're all I have."

They were loaded back into the car and taken to a hamburger place he'd seen commercials about when he lived at home. Going inside, Del picked up Jane when she started to fuss about the little fall she'd taken, and they all found a table.

Almost sick with worry, Todd let someone order for him. Peter sat beside him and let him see a folder he had with him. It was adoption papers. It had not just his name on them, but his sisters', as well as Brian's. Todd asked the big man what that meant.

"Just as Del told you. He and his wife are going to take you home with them as their children. They'll take good care of you, and you'll never have to worry about them giving you away to a place like you're in now, or I'll personally kick their butts. But that's not going to happen. They'll be good parents, and you'll want for nothing." He said all he wanted was a bed and food all the time. "I'm sure you do, son. I'm sure you do. However, there are a lot of things they'll be able to give you that I'm betting you've not had from your parents. Your mother, more than likely, but not your father. They'll both love you all like you're all the candy in the world wrapped into a nice box with a bow."

He couldn't help it. Todd had been trying for so long to be brave for his family, but it was just too much right now. Crying hard, his body shaking with it, it wasn't until he was lifted up and put over a strong shoulder that he knew he was going to be able to talk to Del. They were outside on a bench when he was asked if he was all right.

"Yes, sir. I've been making sure my sisters were all right since Momma died, and I've been scared to death that someone would take them away and I'd never see them again. Then my cousin, who I never seen before, comes along, and I have to take care that he's not hurt either. That woman, she's meaner than a snake and takes our food from us when we're bad." He looked up at Del. "I promise you, if you take my sisters and not me, they'll be as good as gold. Just make sure my father doesn't try and sell them off like he wanted to. He would have, too, if not for the social worker coming by all the time after Momma died. Now we're in this home that I don't know, and we got nothing from our home. I just don't think I'm going to make it. I'm going to have me a heart attack before I can relax again. You understand?"

"I do, and I'm so sorry you've had to go through all that. No seven-year-old should have to be stressed out over keeping his sisters safe. But you've done a good job, Todd. They're very safe, and it's all do to you." Todd thanked him. "Now, later today, we're going to go see the judge about the adoption. We want all four of you, but my wife is going to see if she can find Brian's dad and get him home for him. Also, we're never going to have to worry about your father. I'm going to take care that he understands what he's done is wrong."

"You gonna kill him?" Del didn't answer, and that scared Todd just a little. Then he realized it was all on his father and not him, so he smiled at the big man. "You can beat him up, but if you go to jail, they'll not let us go home with you. And I'd surely like to go there. I don't care what sort of house you have either, so long as we can have a warm bed and some food when we want it. We'll be good too."

"I've figured that out as well." Todd nodded.

"All right. Let's go back in and have some lunch, talk about some of the things you'd like to see in your room when we get home, as well as some of the things you'd like to have for school and such. My mom, Katie, she's wanting a hug too, if you can find it in you to give her one. She's been more worried than you have about the four of you."

"She must have had some really bad dreams then. I know I have." Del told him she'd never tell them that, but she more than likely had. "You're not kidding us, are you, Del? I mean, you're not going to just take us back there and never come back? I'd understand it, I would, but it would hurt badly if you did."

"I'm going to talk to Peter about having you stay with us while we're here. That way, you don't ever have to go back. Then when that meeting is over, you're going to have to brace yourself. I have four more brothers at home and a grandpa of my own, as does Merce. You're going to have so many relatives around you that you might wish you were back at the home."

"Never."

Del nodded at him, and they went back to their seats. His burger and fries were waiting for him as soon as he settled. Taking his first bite of a hot French fry he'd had in forever, it seemed, Todd hoped the man was right. He surely did. It would be nice to have a hot meal all the time again.

Chapter 8

Del didn't so much as stretch as they stood on the front porch of the nice home. He had been warned, no less than ten times, that he was not to hit his cousin no matter how much he provoked him. No one, especially his mom, wanted to visit him in jail. Merce didn't threaten him so much as she glared. He found that to be so much more telling than the threats his family had put on him.

Del wanted to stretch his neck. To feel the tension that was building up behind his eyes dissipate into the evening air with a loud pop. However, just as he was moving his shoulders to just relieve a little of it, he looked at his wife.

There was no mistaking the look she gave him. Merce could outstare his mom right now, he'd bet. Not only that, but he was more afraid of her than he was his mom. Del was terrified of her. So, instead of doing all the things he wanted to the man in this house for what he'd done to his own children, he pushed the doorbell. When it broke under his finger, he didn't bother looking at the rest of them.

"It must have been very old." No one said anything when he said that. He did hear Peter laugh, but it was cut short. He'd bet his last check that his mom had popped him a good one in the back of the head. It was her favorite thing to do when she was upset.

The door opened, and there stood James Pencil. Del wanted to point out that he looked just like his namesake. That his head was pointed at the top, with graying hair that looked like he'd styled it to be messy. Fucker. Putting out his hand, Del had an uncontrollable urge to kill James.

"What did you do?" He looked at Merce when she smacked him. "Del, I believe you were told several times to behave yourself."

Not sure what she was talking about, he looked to where James had been standing, and he was gone. So gone, in fact, that one of his shoes was still where the man had been. Looking around for him, he saw the man lying on the floor across the room, not moving.

"How did he get there?" Del was smacked again, and that seemed to be all it took to loosen up some of his memories. "I did that."

"Of course you did that, you fucker. You grabbed him around the throat, lifted him up, then tossed him across the room. He flew like he had wings. What the hell is wrong with you?" He didn't answer Merce. Not that he didn't have one, but he didn't think it would help matters if he admitted he enjoyed knowing he had tossed the man around a little. "I'll deal with you in a bit. Christ, I hope he doesn't remember how he got there. That way, you might not spend the next fifty or so years in prison."

He didn't follow her in but waited until his mom had passed him. Del was sure she had a grin on her face, but he wasn't going to push his luck. It wasn't until Peter stood in front of him that he was able to smile. Peter just shook his head.

"You beat me to it. And I don't know if you noticed it or not, but Mom had a gun out at her side. Like her thought process was to shoot him right where he stood. So if you think about it, you probably saved his life and kept Mom from going to prison too." Del asked his brother if he was sure it was a gun. "Yes. I'm sure. She not only put it in her purse, Del, but she took out the clip, the ammo in the chamber, as well as put the unspent bullet back in the clip. I had no idea she knew anything about guns. Did you?"

"No. But then she's been a mystery to me all my life." They both laughed as they entered the house. There was enough shrieking going on that he thought about putting his fingers in his ears. Whatever was going on had to do with the new wife and her husband laid out on the floor.

Peter put his fingers in his mouth and whistled. Del had always been jealous of him being able to do that. However, today it didn't seem to have the desired effect as it normally did. The arguing went on for a few more minutes until his mother pulled out the gun and fired it twice toward the windows just beyond them. That worked.

"Now, we're going to have a nice conversation, and you will stop that caterwauling before I have to tape your mouth closed. Go into your dining room and sit down before I have to sit you down." Mom looked at him. "Del, honey, get a bucket of water and dump it on this little shit to have him come around. I'm not sure how much time we have before the others arrive, but we really should be ready."

"Mom, when did you get a gun? And learn how to fire it?" She just stared at him. "I think that's a good question, don't you?"

"I've had it for years. As for how to fire it? Honey, all you need to do is pull the trigger. That's all it takes. Now get the shit up, and we'll get this over with, so I can go home and spoil my grandchildren."

When she walked away, he looked at Peter. He was staring at Mom like he'd never seen her before. Going to the kitchen, he was surprised to see it in such a mess. There didn't seem to be any staff around, nor did it look as if they were in any way cleaning up after themselves.

Getting a large pot off the sink, he filled it with cold water. It had been tempting to use hot, but he thought he'd pushed enough buttons for today. Taking it to the front hall, he was disappointed to see that James had awakened on his own and was headed to the dining room.

Since the front door was open, Judge Middleton walked in with three other men. Two of them were officers, and the third one he didn't know. Also, there were the children. It did his heart a world of good to see them smiling and giving him a hug. Putting down the pot of water, he got down on his knees and hugged all three of them. Brian was at a doctor's appointment and would join them later. They entered the dining room just as Judge Middleton was talking about why they were there.

"We're here to acknowledge that you are the biological father to these three children." As the judge went over the reasons for this meeting, he asked James if he wanted an attorney. When he said yes, he was allotted ten minutes to call himself one and another thirty minutes to have him at the house. Otherwise, he was forfeiting his need for one. James asked if it was still his home. "For now. Your time is running out, young man. I suggest you get your butt in gear."

Twenty-nine minutes had passed when his attorney showed up. He didn't look any happier about it than James did. He must have been at a softball game too. The T-shirt he had on said he was a coach. When the judge brought him up to date on what was going on, Mr. Shadow looked at his client.

"I'm sorry. What does he mean, you gave your children up for adoption?" James told him he was beginning a new life. "Without your children? Do you have any idea the repercussions that could come with this?"

"So long as they're no longer my problem, I don't care." Middleton handed some paperwork to Shadow. When he read it over, he looked shocked, more so than before. "You said you didn't care what happened to them so long as they weren't in your hair? How the hell do you think that is even remotely a good thing?"

James leaned over to Shadow and whispered loud enough for them all to hear his plan. "I'm not sure we've spoken about this, but my dead wife made it so only the kids could collect the money. However, if anything should happen to them that they're no longer my children, the money would be given to charity. I'm working on this one thing at a time. After this, I'm going to declare she wasn't of sound mind when she said that."

Shadow looked at him, and Del spoke then. "I'm here to adopt the children so they won't be in the system. I'm their blood relative through my mom. Her sister was James the dick's mother." Shadow looked at his mom before looking back at him. "Her name is Katherine Archer. You should have received information on her through an email that was sent out on Monday."

"I got it but didn't know what was going on until this moment. I'm sorry about that. I know who you are. As well as your wealth." He looked back at his client. "I'm no longer your attorney, Mr. Pencil. I can't do this for you, whatever it is you think I might be able to do. You've dug your own hole, and now you're going to be buried in it. I'm not going to lose my license because your wife was a good deal smarter than you ever gave her credit for."

"I need that money so I can start fresh." Shadow told him good luck. "You're my attorney, Phillip. I demand that you fix this so I don't have to wait any longer for the money that should have been mine all along."

"Your Honor, I want to say that I had no dealings with this monstrosity. Nor did I have any involvement in Mr. Pencil giving up his children. I would like to suggest that if it is something the Archers are willing to take on, they should most assuredly be able to adopt and care for these children. They'd be better off with them than with a man who has no concept of what having a family means."

"I agree with you, Mr. Shadow. As soon as we're finished with the rest of this meeting, for lack of a better term, we'll see to it that they're in a good home." Todd raised his hand and asked if they were going to have to go back to the home. "No. You're going to go home with these good people. I know we've spoken about this, but I want to ask you again. Are you all right with spending your life with this family?"

"Yes, sir. Yesterday we had some really good food. And when I was upset, crying, Del held me until I was okay again." James called his son a pussy. Before he could react, Merce punched him in the face, and he fell back off his chair and landed on the floor. "My goodness, sir, they sure do know how to make a boy feel like we're safe, don't you think?"

"I do at that. And had Mrs. Archer not hit him, I'm sure any number of people would have done it." Judge Middleton looked at them. "You can leave if you wish. The rest of this is going to be having Mr. Pencil and his wife here put in jail pending the trial for what they've done by endangering children. Thank you for this. Also, I will need you to be here when we talk about young Brian with his mother."

"I have some information on that case, Your Honor." Peter handed him what he'd been able to find. "It seems his wife has called in a couple of favors and had her ex-husband detained in Grenada pending a stolen identification. She has been playing him, keeping him away from his son so she can do what her brother has done. Give them to the home, so she no longer has to deal with him. There is also an indication that she had her lover break the young man's leg in order to keep him from interrupting their…fun time, I'm going to call it."

Del and his new family headed out the door. He didn't know what was going to happen to James and his wife, but he found that he didn't care. Kissing Merce's bruised knuckles, he told her he loved her.

"I love you as well. How about we load up the

kids, head to the hospital to get Brian, and go home. I don't know about you, but I've had enough of your family for the time being." He agreed with her. "Good. All right, guys. Load your butts into the car. We're off to home."

The kids were still cheering as they pulled up in front of the hospital. Calling ahead to see if Brian was finished, he was happy that he was. The judge had given them temporary care of Brian until his father returned, and that was fine with them. The kids didn't know each other any more than he did them, but they were making a good start in getting to be close friends.

"You know we're going to have to tangle with Mary soon enough." He said he didn't care for now. "I don't either, but we're going to have to do the same thing all over."

"This time, we'll have a good solid lead on getting his dad home. I'm all right with that too." She said she was going to miss the little boy. "Not if we can talk his dad into living closer to us. I'm sure it won't be all that hard after we tell him how hard we worked on getting his son safe."

"You're a dork." He kissed her again. "I love you, Del, but there are times I do worry about your sanity.

Before You Go...

HELP AN AUTHOR

write a review

THANK YOU!

Share your voice and help guide other readers to these wonderful books. Even if it's only a line or two, your reviews help readers discover the author's books so they can continue creating stories that you'll love. Log in to your favorite retailer and leave a review. Thank you.

AWARD WINNING, BESTSELLING AUTHOR

Kathi Barton, a winner of the Pinnacle Book Achievement award as well as a best-selling author on Amazon and All Romance books, lives in Nashport, Ohio, with her husband, Paul. When not creating new worlds and romance, Kathi and her husband enjoy camping and going to auctions. She can also be seen at county fairs with her husband, who is an artist and potter.

Her muse, a cross between Jimmy Stewart and Hugh Jackman, brings her stories to life for her readers in a way that has them coming back time and again for more. Her favorite genre is paranormal romance, with a great deal of spice. You can visit Kathi online and drop her an email if you'd like. She loves hearing from her fans. aaronskiss@gmail.com.

Follow Kathi on her blog: http://kathisbartonauthor. blogspot.com/

www.ingramcontent.com/pod-product-compliance
Lightning Source LLC
Chambersburg PA
CBHW030226180626
46810CB00008B/2984